WITH
A PINCH
OF SALT...

WITH
A PINCH
OF SALT...

Jas Anand

Srishti
PUBLISHERS & DISTRIBUTORS

SRISHTI PUBLISHERS & DISTRIBUTORS
N-16, C. R. Park
New Delhi 110 019
editorial@srishtipublishers.com

First published by
Srishti Publishers & Distributors in 2014

Typeset by Eshu Graphic

Acknowledgements

I would like to begin by thanking you for picking up the book of a first time author. Hope it tickles your funny bone. I have a long list of people to thank in this journey leading up to the publishing of this book.

Indispensables

Deepest gratitude and thankfulness to my parents for all that they have unconditionally done for me in all these years. Big thanks to my wife Nazneen for being a pillar of support and to our two lovely boys Aman and Ryan for illuminating our lives. I would like to also thank my sister Mona for always being there for me.

Catalysts

A first time author is like a school boy entering a chemistry lab for the very first time. It takes a series of experiments before you can freeze your style of narration. During these phases of experimentation, four friends had been particularly supportive and also displayed high degree of tolerance – Natasha Kapoor for setting the pace, Heena Patel and Rohit Bhargava during the middle patch and Vishal Maru particularly towards the completion of the book. Vishal Maru has also been party to some of these real life anecdotes which have inspired this piece of fiction.

I would also like to thank author and corporate trainer Priya Kumar for putting me across to Sohin Lakhani of Embassy books. Sohin was the one who guided me to approach Srishti for this book. He believed that Srishti had the ideal platform and distribution for this genre.

Ecosystem

The book is a slice of life and is modelled on humour from everyday settings. Friends and colleagues hence are the most pivotal part of life. I want to extend a sincere thanks to all my friends – right from college days to all my close colleagues in various offices.

Sounding Board

Apart from the catalysts mentioned above, I had done intensive test marketing with lots of friends/colleagues before embarking upon the final manuscript. I am indebted to all my friends who took their valuable time out to give their inputs. Some of them had to bear with tacky initial drafts. Your contribution has been immense in giving the final shape to the book. I would like to thank Saurabh Makhija, Sameer Gupte, Samar Banwat, Rajan Bodh, Rajneesh Chaturvedi, Urvashi Krishan, Manish Jaiswal, Indu Das, Arnab Das, Manish Arora, Puneet Arora, Reshma Nath, Amita Nene, Amita Sharma, Divya Pinge, Ruchi Jain, Sangram Bhalla and B. Vijay Kumar for their feedback.

Believers

The entire process would have been a waste if Srishti Publishers had not shown faith in this project. I extend my most sincere gratitude to the entire team at Srishti to take this project past the finishing line.

And last but not the least, I would like to extend my sincere thanks and appreciation to Leean for the catchy cover design.

I welcome you to the world of unique characters and funny anecdotes...served with a pinch of salt.

Chapter 1

Introduction to the book

Life is a perpetual series of anecdotes, one after the other. If you see with an open mind and creative eyes, there are unique characters all around us leading to innumerable anecdotes and memorable stories to tell.

Just like you need a telescope to see a star far away in the galaxy, you need to observe, absorb and enjoy our surroundings to see anecdotes all around (or we can simply call it 'The Human Microscope'). Once you start seeing them regularly, it can actually be an uplifting discovery. A good friend of mine once told me, 'it is difficult to find men with honour and equally difficult to find men with humour'. The men with humour are the ones who see these stories bubbling all over the place.

Let us set some ground rules in the beginning itself.

Ground rule no.1: Carry 'The Human Microscope' everyday with you to discover humour bubbling around you.

Ground rule no. 2: Every person around you is a 'potential character' (or a 'prospect' as per the sales lingo). Our job is to observe everything suspiciously and be relentless till we discover something funny in them. These funny traits are known as 'tendencies'.

Ground rule no. 3: Once you can spot 'characters' and 'tendencies', the anecdotes are inevitable to come.

Ground rule no. 4: Once you have a fantastic collection of 'characters' and 'anecdotes', there is bound to be enough humour and happiness in your life. Additionally, it also gives an extra edge during various parties to tell your funny stories.

Ground rule no. 5: Most importantly, it is not just humour, each character offers so much to learn in terms of 'what to do' and 'what not to do'.

Ground rule no. 6: If you have enough stories, even an idiot like me can churn out a book from them. Apart from regular dosage of humour, there are several strategic advantages too.

The book is simple - it is a collection of numerous unique characters I have come across in my life and some anecdotes related to them or related to their tendencies. Some people have idiosyncrasies that make them really 'out of the crowd'. In other words, the book is about everyday humour and it makes that a 'slice of life'. The work is still a piece of fiction; the inspiration is drawn from multiple sources that have been merged / integrated to give it a readable form.

A roving eye for a little bit of fun makes life more joyous and de-stresses you from time to time. As readers we do not like bland stuff and hence I have added a dash of spices with a pinch of salt. Very often, when bored to death or when trapped in meaningless situation (read boring weddings, boring parties, and boring meetings), the ability to see unique characters and unique stories makes life interesting.

I have 3 major disclaimers at the outset – 1. I could not include all characters - *just not possible* in one book (so, there is a strong case for a sequel as well). 2. The collection of anecdotes is not exhaustive; it is a random sampling from each of the characters that have been shortlisted (So what about the remaining stories? Well, that's another reason for a sequel). 3. It is a piece of fiction inspired by the bustling life around me.

As a writer, I am happy with the characters I have chosen. As a manager, I am glad that there is enough scope for a sequel. As readers, I hope you find it funny and enjoyable.

Let's cut our preface, introduction and foreword right here, and let the characters and anecdotes take over.

Lights; roll camera; action!

CHAPTER 2

Closer look at idiosyncrasies or tendencies

This chapter contains the crux of spotting everyday humour. All of us have some idiosyncrasies, or simply tendencies which are uniquely funny. In some of us these idiosyncrasies are subtle, while in others they are very strong. Most of the time, these tendencies are latent and come alive in 'specific situations'; whereas a few persons have tendencies which are consistently present 24*7. In fact, the latter are indeed a rare breed as their server never needs a shut down and their set up operates at consistently high capacity utilization. Such characters normally catch the eye of most people and become a hot topic of discussion when friends gather around the coffee machine in the offices or whenever anecdotes are being told. These are obvious buffoons; difficult to be missed. These individuals are typical 'stereotypes' and one can pre-empt their reactions in many situations.

The second variety is a smarter breed and they can often walk away spotless unless we make an attempt to spot them. Actually spotting them is also very easy; all one needs is a fine skill of observation and a laundry list of 'specific situations' when humans behave in a peculiar fashion. Very often I have seen that it is in specific situations that such tendencies tend to come out in the open more rampantly. These people belong to the, "Microscopic Moron," variety. It is not very different from the 'cause and effect' theory. I know it is getting too theoretical; let me give some examples of situations when people behave differently:

- First time business meetings: The first business meeting with anyone on earth can be an interesting opportunity. I have been able to observe at least fifteen ways of how people exchange business cards. The most peculiar mechanism is when the donor of the card uses both his hands to bring the card (placed horizontally) up exactly to a midway level between his stomach and chest; bends the back by 22 degrees while managing simultaneously to push his neck out and successfully oozing an expression which has pseudo smile or a pseudo chuckle depending upon the situation. While the larger fact is still that 95 times out of 100, the card exchange will be normal; there would be 5 times when you come up with some funny findings. As the meeting proceeds, you will very often see a great pretence of very intense hearing being offered to your words suitably synchronized with adequate nodding of head to reinforce the spirit of attentive listening. The oscillation of the head gets more and more turbulent as the meeting progresses, obviously to camouflage the inattentiveness. These are usually people, "who have mentally left the room", however they have deputed a highly oscillating head to take care of the physical proceedings. There are many more possibilities of what might happen in a first time meeting. All I am trying to put forward is a concept of 'specific situation' and various responses you might see.

- Another specific situation is to observe a differentiated behaviour of boys when they are "alone" vis-a-vis "boys along with girls" situation. Boys are very different when they are with girls. This tendency is active largely during mid-teens going up to college days. The tendency tends to fizzle out as one grows older. Imagine two guys in college getting bored to death together and are unable to find any reason to feel excited, energized or purposeful. In case you air drop a beautiful girl in the middle of this monotony; you will find that energy will be back at a speed you can't imagine. Things change at a pace faster than 100 metres Olympic race with both the guys attempting to outdo each other to impress the girl.

- This one is risky, but I must put to perspective what I observe, my wife becomes a changed woman whenever she enters a shopping mall. It is like Abracadabra; a magical transformation takes place. All the worries disappear and life comes to a state of perfect bliss. However, when we step back into the car, there will be a sudden clash of thunder (an opposite reaction to Abracadabra) and she will recall all the worries about the driver leaving the job, maid giving her trouble or worry for our son's school admission. I have learnt by experience that the most suitable time to nag your husband is when he is held captive inside the car and especially if he is driving. He is all yours and you can go on till your "cup of complaints is empty". Wives can send me hate mails for exposing this trick and husbands can send me sympathies.

- Movie premieres are very typical situations where courtesy takes clear importance over truth. I have attended a couple of premiers and trust me, both the movies were horrendous. Horrendous is an understatement, they were probably the most outstanding disasters of the year. The human idiosyncrasy of being courteous and not hurting the film maker comes out to the fore in such situations. It is understandable that you may not want to hurt the film maker; however people forget where to draw the line. Instead of being courteous, people tend to become aggressively appreciative with words like "Blockbuster", "Super hit", "Excellent" being heard all around. The situation mentioned above is very easily comprehensible. I observe that such situation is prevalent in everyday life, albeit on a lower scale or magnitude. Sometimes bosses come up with quite senseless ideas during strategy meets or business reviews which many employees choose to appreciate despite not really being convinced. And in fact, on some of the occasions, those ideas end up getting implemented as the staff had chosen to give more importance to courtesy over truth or courage.

These are a few situations that I have elaborated to get your mind oriented to the trick of observing situations. In this book I have compiled some funny characters and individuals that I have encountered in my life and have put anecdotes directly related to them or related to the idiosyncrasy that they transmit.

The idiosyncrasies could be many; I have covered the few that I found most interesting. The word 'idiosyncrasy' has negative connotation, so I will use the word 'tendency' for giving it the due respect. Anything that leads to humour is something very valuable.

I have divided the book in the following sections:
Section 1 – Stupidity and its derivatives
Section 2 – Matter of hearts
Section 3 – Mind, intelligentsia and pseudo appeal
Section 4 – Titbits

Section 1

Stupidity and its derivatives

Simon "Satellite"

If you ask him his name, he might tell you that he is a mechanical engineer. If you ask him his qualifications, he might just tell you that Bill Gates was a school dropout and qualifications do not matter. Just in case you still have some patience left, and ask him what then really matters, he will probably tell you to read a holy book and know it for yourself.

He could never answer to the point or rather he was always a few miles away from the answer you were searching. I used to call him a "satellite" who kept orbiting around the topic but never came to the point. The bigger problem with him was that his problem didn't end here. On certain days he was capable of going on a major negativity trip and found faults with everything on earth. Theoretically speaking, if he was a one man jury for a Miss Universe contest, I would not be surprised that there was no winner at all in that year.

The problem with him was that his problem still did not end there. Simon believed that there was something always working towards pulling him down. In my personal opinion, he was already seven feet below the ground; so any one who wanted to pull him down further would have to a dig a hole deeper than that. People, cartels or conspirators usually do not have the inclination to dig such deep holes especially if the person in question is Simon "Satellite".

Very often there are long queues outside Bank ATMs mainly because there are some people who believe in counting the notes before they leave and then there are others who do the counting twice to recheck their own counting. Simon would fall into the twice counting category.

Special Features and tendencies:

- Natural satellite. Perpetually beats around the bush (can't come to the point unless shaken and stirred)
- His thoughts are always in a state of Brownian Motion
- Always hyper
- Always on high alert (no amount of conspiracy will work; he is forever planning a combat strategy to counter all possible attacks from all corners)

He could have done the Indian Army proud, but he chose an easy way out by becoming a manager. I am sure he must be spreading a lot of humor, "unknowingly and unintentionally", somewhere in corporate India. Not just that, he must be having some serious complaints about how bad the corporate world is. And his bosses and his team mates must be hoping to develop a sign language to deal with him in a direct and crisp manner.

(Just for the sake of information, we did our MBA together many years back.)

The Satellite Effect

While it is quite comprehensible what to expect when dealing with Simon, to make matters clear I have reproduced some of the typical interactions that took shape with him. The overall feeling of frustration and irritation caused during interactions with him can be loosely referred to as the "Satellite Effect."

Definition of Satellite Effect: "It is a deeply irritating feeling caused by a whirlpool of words which seem to be floating forever on the orbit like a satellite, but never tend to converge into anything meaningful."

Simon is not the only person who creates this "Satellite Effect". During my stint as a corporate manager I have seen many management consultants who when asked very direct objective questions will give the entire "spectrum of macroeconomic information", excepting the one you were looking for. Some of these management consultants have a unique flair to draw unnecessary 3*3 matrices and take the topic to a different direction. Sometimes I feel that some of these management consultants should be rechristened as 'management satellites'.

Now coming back to Simon, I am reproducing a few real interactions below that would occur when he is around in your vicinity.

Satellite Effect No. 1

Me: Simon, what is the time?

Simon Satellite: Time! This is the most horrible time of my life. My father is not sending me money, I can't understand any damn thing in the lectures, no girl ever seems to be interested in me and the hostel food is pathetic.

Me (Literally shaking and stirring him): Simon I just wanted to know the exact time in your watch.

Simon Satellite: Watch! You call this a watch. This is a piece of junk I picked up from the roadside. It is made in China and I don't know how long Chinese products like this will last.

Me (with lots of irritation and firmness): Exact time please.

Simon Satellite: It is 10.15 a.m.

If I hadn't exercised firmness, the discussion could have shifted to Swiss watches and from there probably to tourism in Switzerland and may be to the black money of Indian politicians lying in Swiss Bank accounts. With Simon "Satellite" you have to be on your guard and push for closures.

Satellite Effect No. 2

Me: Simon, let's go to the canteen and have food.

Simon: You get the worst possible food in this hostel. If you want to enjoy food, you must come with me to Delhi. I will take you for the most sumptuous kebabs that you would ever eat in your life. Why just kebabs, you get the most awesome street food in Delhi. Even Chinese tourists have specially started coming from Shanghai to have Chinese food in Delhi.

Me (Interrupting him before he names all the cuisines that his limited general knowledge may acknowledge): Lunch? Have you eaten or should I go to the mess?

Simon: This mess is truly a mess. If you want to see a mess, you must come with me to the officer's mess in New Delhi cantonment. I love army cantonments. The roads are so well maintained and the greenery is awesome.

Irrespective of his mannerisms, New Delhi is certainly a fantastic place for food lovers and Army cantonments are indeed well maintained.

Satellite Effect No. 3

Situation: There was a notice in the hostel to make a contribution of fifty rupees for flood victims. I was relaxing in the TV lounge without my wallet (which was in my room) when I saw Simon giving fifty rupees to the hostel caretaker. I just thought of borrowing the same amount from Simon right away and make my contribution as well (just to close the loop on this one).

Me: Hey Simon, do you have some extra money? Please make a contribution on my behalf and I will pay you back later.

Simon: Money! I had lots of money; full five thousand rupees, I gave one thousand to the canteen, I bought books for two thousand, repaired my bike for thousand bucks, made an international call to my brother in Manchester, which is 200 km north of London for 500 rupees. Now I hardly have any money left with me. By the way, my bro is a software engineer with a fortune 500 company and has gone to Manchester for a project. In fact, it is the first time my brother has gone abroad. He has fallen in love with cleanliness of Manchester and is also bowled over by the beautiful girls in that city. Look at our college, there are hardly any pretty girls around and the few that we have, don't even know of my existence.

Me: (Shaking and stirring him) I just need fifty rupees right now and will give it back the moment I step into my room

Simon: Oh! 50 rupees, of course, please take it.

Satellite effect no. 4

Situation: Imagine that Simon Satellite has to confess his love to a girl. Let us call her Suzie for convenience. So Simon calls Suzie up to invite her for a coffee date.

Simon: Hello Suzie! How are you?

Suzie: I am fine. How about you?

Simon: Fine! I paid a fine of a hundred rupees for wrong parking. There was no board which said 'no parking'. Nothing is fine in this country.

Suzie: Have you called to discuss the problems of the country?

Simon: Country! There are more than two hundred countries across the globe. Each country has its own problem. Let us discuss Afghanistan today. It is alphabetically correct to start with 'A'. What do you say?

Suzie: Listen Simon! I am not interested in Afghanistan or any of the other 199 countries. You wanted to meet me to discuss something important. What is that you want to discuss?

Simon: Discussion! The art of discussion is dying down. This is the era of debates and arguments. Look at news channels; they always have something to debate about. Discussions are passé.

Suzie: Simon! It is really difficult to have a focused discussion with you over phone. Let us meet and talk. How about coffee?

Simon: Now *that* is big business in countries like Ethiopia and Kenya. Well coffee also reminds me that I had called to meet you for a cup of coffee.

Suzie: I am so glad that you faintly remember it. Where exactly do you want to meet?

Simon: Exactly! What do you mean by exactly? Do you want to know the place in terms of latitude and longitude?

Suzie: Only name and place would be enough.

Frustrated by now, Suzie hangs up the phone and the confession of love is pending till today. Suzie has moved on in life and married Suzuki and they have a happy family full of little Suzuki's and little Suzies.

> **If you ever find him:** Please don't ask him any question.

Stage Hijacked

It was 13th August, which clearly meant 15th August was not far away. And it takes no great mathematics to calculate that 2 days just have 48 hours. It was too short a period for Vishal, Simon and me to think of an absolutely new script for the college play. For all "non Indians" and the ones with "weak general knowledge", India celebrates its Independence Day on August 15. Vishal was one of my closest college friends. Modesty aside for a while, it will not be an exaggeration to say that we were rock stars of our college. Not in the musical sense of the word, but in the sense of popularity and extracurricular activities. We were out of town for one whole week to attend an important marriage and Debodutta seized this opportunity and took control of the annual play for Independence Day celebrations in our college.

Now who is Debodutta?

Well, in some hidden corner of his heart, Debodutta Paul was an aspiring director waiting to come out in the public eye. Aspirations can be funny; sometimes they have no correlation with reality. All this while, our towering presence in the college did not allow him to realize his hidden aspiration. He was quick to latch on to this chance just as a crocodile attacks his prey in a jiffy. However, some joys are often meant to be short-lived; this was a big lesson that Debodutta Paul was going to learn on August 15.

As a part of temporary reality, Debodutta was in command and was indeed directing the play while we unfortunately had no real role in it. After swallowing a lot of pride, we decided to approach Debodutta for a small role. Our popularity could have taken a major beating if we didn't enter the stage at all that year. A voluntary 'guest appearance' was offered by us.

Me: I heard that you have finalized the script for the play.

Debodutta: Yeah, it is going to be a fantastic play, you guys could have played some important role in it if you had been in town earlier.

Vishal: Your wish can still come true. We are volunteering for a 'guest appearance'.

Debodutta: You guys have a good sense of humour, but now the play is finalized and there are hardly two days left. It will be difficult to accommodate you now.

Vishal: Where there is a will, there is a way.

Me: What is the play about?

Debodutta: Patriotism. The struggle to attain freedom during the pre-independence era.

Vishal: There is good news for you; your play has just got a facelift. We have decided to voluntarily add few scenes to your play and to make your life simpler. We have also decided to act them out as well.

Simon: I am making myself available for the play too. I can give a short introduction about the play and then get lost.

He knew that we could be bad bullies, so he agreed with great reluctance like most fathers do when their daughters decide to marry a guy they don't approve of.

"Just one scene each, only for you guys. I would have not even accommodated Robert De Niro, but I can't say no to you guys," Debodutta clarified the extent of his accommodating spirit.

"Done!" All three of us echoed in a synchronized roar.

I almost felt as terrifying as Osama Bin Laden. Nevertheless, the play was on.

Since it was a college play, there were other actors too in the play (who were our good friends); so we decided to accept the one scene offer. The intention was not to hurt our other friends and sabotage their hard work and practice. The one scene formula was thus a fair and congenial compromise from both sides.

The play did not require a narrator, but suddenly it got one. And the narrator happened to be Simon Satellite. The person who always had trouble with speaking in short had a daunting task ahead for him.

To accommodate the three of us, I added two scenes right at the beginning of the play. The first scene was a brief introduction by a narrator and that was followed by a scene in an Indian house which intended to depict a growing unrest in the Indian youth and hence showed them gearing up for the protests against the British administration.

Debodutta was very happy that we were fairly reasonable in our approach. The negotiated amendments made to the play are reproduced word by word as below:

Narrator (to be played by Simon Satellite): It was an era of mutiny; it was the time when the young Indians wanted independence at any cost. Let us have a look at one such Indian household and how they were ready to play a part for the country.

Scene: I would run into the house.

Me: Did you hear, the police has lathi charged our beloved leader Lala Lajpat Rai? Come, let us rush there.

Sandeep (My brother in the play and the original hero as per Debodutta's script): Let us go quickly to the spot; it is a shame that they have done this.

Vishal: (playing the role of our old and frail father): Go boys, my best wishes are with you.

After this additional scene, the play shifts to the original plot where the hero (Sandeep) was supposed to attend the procession in support of the great Lala Lajpat Rai. The entire addition to the play was very marginal and fitted into the rest of the script very comfortably.

Everyone was satisfied with the deal we had made, particularly Debodutta. The bulk of his creativity was retained and the joy was evident on his face; it was almost like an orgasm for him.

The practice sessions were held and things seemed in control and in smooth continuity. BUT, it was always going to be very difficult for lead actors like us to accept "one line" roles.

One night prior to the play, while the three of us were having beer, we had a change of heart.

"'One scene seems too short and stupid to me. We are popular guys in college and have some reputation to care for," I planted the seed of a conspiracy.

"I agree," said Vishal.

"Let us add a few lines. A little bit of random histrionics will make our presence on stage more impactful," I gave my suggestion

"Good idea. Let us do that," replied Vishal

"I am a narrator and I need some space to throw the point across. I am feeling very handicapped with one line narration." Simon too seemed to echo our sentiments.

It was trilaterally decided that we would add some lines and histrionics directly on the stage without informing Debodutta. From "One line role", we decided to make it a one paragraph role. Each person was given liberty to be his own dialogue writer for the enhanced role. And this was the big lacuna that Vishal and I did not address. Having known the tendency of Simon Satellite, the situation demanded prudence, which we did not exercise.

"Cheers to the play!"

It was fair in our opinion. Why should only Debodutta get an orgasm?

15th August, 1999, the day of the play
The play begins

Simon Satellite the narrator (with an extremely anguished look, to the extent that it could be classified as blatant overacting):

India was once known as the Golden Bird. There are more than 10,000 types of birds in the world. Parrots are green, swans are white, crows are black, but India was golden. It was a golden bird with a golden history. And nobody can deny that gold is a precious commodity. But the birds can fly freely and independently in the sky. The eagles fly high while seagulls don't fly so high. But

India was colonized by the British. The golden bird could not fly freely.

The Indian youth was angry. It was an era of mutiny, an era when the Indians were ready to die for their country. It was a time to do or die. The youth was ready for all kinds of sacrifices; they just had one vision and one dream – to see an independent India. They wanted to see that golden bird flying high in the sky once again. While the crows might die, the eagles might die, a martyr lives forever in the hearts of everyone. India produced many such brave hearts from Bhagat Singh to Veer Savarkar, from Chandrashekhar Azad to Subhash Chandra Bose. Indian history will always glitter due to the contributions made by these bravehearts. Mel Gibson also directed a movie called Braveheart but it had nothing to do with Indian independence. It is unfortunate that Mel Gibson did not focus on independence struggle in India but here we are doing what Mel Gibson did not.

Simon went totally out of control vigorously moving his hands and legs all over the stage and the narrator (who was supposed to stand still at one place) was swaying like an angry pendulum from left to right and back again. Bottom-line, one paragraph role turned into a 2 page role with his trademark "satellite effect" with descriptions of different types of birds and detailed biography of the legendary Mel Gibson.

What happened next was the most deadly cascading effect you would ever get to see. Each role got enhanced on the spot by various actors and it was one of the most exponential trajectories of role growth you can imagine.

Me: Sandeep, you are sitting peacefully in the house, are you even aware that our beloved leader Lala Lajpat Rai has been hit with lathis during the procession? How dare they do this to him!

They will have to pay the price for this. I am not going to pardon them. I am rushing there and will show what an Indian can do when he loses his cool. Save your lives, run for your lives, because I am not going to spare anyone who comes my way today. Vande Mataram, Inquilab Zindabad.

It was my turn to go berserk and very soon it became a one page role too.

The best U turn came from Vishal, who was originally supposed to play the role of our old and frail father, who could barely manage to lift his hand to bless us.

Vishal: Don't worry boys; your brave father will take revenge for the disrespect shown to our leader. Follow me, I will lead this revolt. Even at the age of 65, I have enough guts to show the British forces what an Indian old man can do when he is angry. It is my turn to prove how deadly I can get.

It was total chaos with all three of us going out of control and totally out of the script. After that scene, the entire play became an extempore and everyone ensured that they spent maximum possible time on the stage. The focus shifted from original lines to maximum "talk time" on the stage.

The twenty-minutes-long play went on till one hour. (Had we known this earlier we could have got our play sponsored by a telecom company who could have proudly advertized "get maximum talk time - much more than you can ever imagine")

Debodutta Paul decided never to direct a play again in his life and instead pursued a career in financial services. I am glad that he has at least become an Investment Director in a private equity firm. He carries the word "Director" in his business card and flaunts it in everyday life; however, I usually avoid investing my money in the funds he manages. I am mindful that one trigger can change the course of his investment. Unmet aspirations can be hounding. It is 13 years since we have finished our college, but whenever we meet over drinks he makes it a point to recollect the horrors of the play that was hijacked thanks to the opening spell of "Simon Satellite".

Chapter 4 (A)

Googly Gilbert

When one flips a coin, one really does not know what will be the outcome. There are two sides and two clear possibilities called heads or tails. If this coin theoretically had an ability to turn into a man, then the specie you will get will be called as Googly Gilbert. Googly Gilbert had two distinct and diverse personalities. He was like the comical reincarnation of Dr. Jekyll and Mr. Hyde.

Gilbert reminded me of the Metrological department that could conveniently defend excess rainfall and drought with equal ease, irrespective of their earlier predictions. In the morning, he could appear as the most pessimistic person in the world with worries ranging from global recession, a horrible boss and absence of a bonafide girl friend. By the evening, he could transform into a multimillionaire play boy who could only see roses on land and rainbows in the sky.

Which one was the real one? I still don't know. Both his acts looked equally convincing. If there was an Oscar for 'day to day' real life performances, then we have a strong nominee here for a lifetime achievement award.

I encountered this character when I was in college (read

MBA days), while he was at that point a reasonably well-employed executive with about five years of work experience and a decent salary. The friendship was very symbiotic; he wanted companions to booze in the night and we (being students) were always on a lookout for an opportunity at a subsidized price. Boy's hostel was the venue for most of our round table conferences (not to be implied literally!).

Indian Films very often have the lead actors playing double roles which are diametrically extreme, where one guy is a simpleton and the other is fairly evolved. Gilbert was one such "double role character" bundled into a single body.

Was he a Schizophrenic? I still don't know. But one thing is sure, that one common thread during his flip-flop was large scale consumption of alcohol.

Special features and tendencies
- Highly nocturnal
- Carries a whisky bottle with him, 9 times out of 10. Whisky is an allegation, it used to be scotch (premium product for college goers).
- Most importantly, a perfectly split personality – Mr. X before drinks; Mr. Y after a few pegs.
- Quintessential politician who thrived on changing sides.
- He was like a calendar which had a new day each day and new month each month.
- He glorified the ultimate question, whether the hen came first or the egg? In his case it would be whether I met the real person in the morning or in the night?

Meeting him over drinks was like meeting two different persons at one time. First few hours you spend with the first person and the latter part with an altogether new person. Physically both continued to be one.

His wife would probably never have extra marital affairs; he would provide her all the variety in shape of one man.

> **If you ever find him**: Don't have drinks with him

Chapter 4 (B)

Poor Little Gregory Gilbert

It was one of those regular dull evenings which all guys without girlfriends have to face day after day, till Gilbert dropped in with a bottle of whisky. Actually, it needs more elaboration: Gilbert was back after a brief IT project in London and he actually walked in with a bottle of Chivas Regal 18 years old. Scotch was a definite luxury in college days, accordingly the room was shut tight and just three persons (including Gilbert and yours truly) were given the access rights to the bottle of Chivas Regal.

A Good friend of mine once said, "Never leave a job unaccomplished". I don't know what exactly he meant by that, but we did well to finish off the entire one liter bottle in one hour flat.

I felt like a helium balloon, flying high and touching the roof. The going was good till we saw Gilbert, nearly in tears. The tears were pretty strategic (not yet flowing) but eyes were pretty full; I was anticipating the flow of those gentle tears in the next ten seconds. And I was so right; a few calculated tear drops fell down from the eyes, sliding past the cheeky (derived from cheeks) corridors.

Vishal (The third person in the room and the frail father of the "stage hijack" story): What's the matter dude?

Gilbert: (with a body language of a martyr, pretending to be very strong): Nothing, nothing at all!

Me: There is something for sure, please tell us.

Gilbert: Nothing buddies. Some pains are too personal to be shared.

The matter was either getting too serious or too melodramatic.

Vishal: You have to tell us, unless you think we are not your good friends

Gilbert: Gregory Gilbert. Poor little Gregory Gilbert.

Me: Poor little Gregory Gilbert? Now who is he?

Gilbert: (with eyes becoming like glaciers and tears flowing like a river): Gregory Gilbert, the poor little boy.

Gilbert: Gregory Gilbert, he is just five years old!

Vishal (worried look): But, who is he?

Gilbert: That poor little boy lives in an orphanage in Shimla. The boy does not even know that his father is alive and is boozing heavily right now in some other part of India.

Guys, you don't know this, nor can you imagine, but I am the father of that poor little boy, Gregory Gilbert. I am that unlucky father.

It was very shocking to hear this since we thought he was a bachelor (in fact we were sure, we once even had a debate on love marriage vs. arranged marriage), it seemed like a bolt from the blue.

Me: But, when did you get married?

Gilbert: It is a long story, the worst part is that I can't even go and tell him that I am his father. It is a long painful story.

Sorry guys, for screwing your evening with my sad and ugly past.

Vishal: Stop it, my respect for you has gone up many folds today. I never knew that a jolly good fellow like you can be fighting such demons.

Me: Really sorry to know this, but what happened? Why can't you pull him out of the orphanage? You are earning well and you can put him to a boarding school. Where is his mother?

Gilbert: It is a long story, I can't do that; if I could, I would have already done that. (Howling like a baby.) I will tell you the whole thing tomorrow morning, when I am in better control of my emotions.

We just hugged him and put him to sleep in our hostel room. It was an extremely low feeling for us and I remember the whole night I was just trying to figure out what could be his issue? Where is the mother? Why should a child of a senior software engineer be struggling in an orphanage? His family was very affluent, why is the child not with the grandparents? There were many unanswered questions.

Sun is a tireless workaholic and very soon it was a new day. The new day started off on a lazy and low note. I made bed tea for Googly Gilbert (can you believe it?); such is the power of human compassion. Not just tea, I offered bread and butter for breakfast, that's usually the best you can expect in a hostel and it could even be interpreted as a seven course meal under the available infrastructure.

Gilbert looked mighty pleased with my hospitality; the appreciation was visible in his eyes.

Me: What's the matter? Why can't you take custody of Gregory?

Gilbert (looking puzzled): Who is Gregory?

Me: Gregory Gilbert, the poor little boy.

Gilbert (perplexed by now, and not just puzzled): Gregory Gilbert? Who the hell is he?

Me: Your son.

Gilbert: Are you mad? I have no son, never married, never fucked – still a virgin.

I was speechless, how can someone be so diametrically opposite in a matter of few hours? I was also surprised that he was still a virgin.

That was the first day we witnessed the Mr. X / Mr. Y effect from Googly Gilbert. During the course of our MBA, we saw Mr. Y taking prominence a few more times. The next time, Mr. Y took over, there were some people who were seriously concerned. The cycle of human compassion got repeated once again, there was bed tea and breakfast for him yet again, but of course I never played the host again. History helps.

His stories were always super tragic ranging from death to divorces, from pain to poverty, from heartaches to heart attacks.

Heart attack reminds me of another story in which he was supposed to get married to a girl as good as it can get. In fact, I never knew if such perfect girls ever existed in this world. The way he described her, most poets would love to make her their inspiration. She was 10 on10 in every aspect of life. But then his stories had a clear cut format, the bride had a heart attack on the day of their marriage and she died in his arms; in front of a thousand guests.

Long live Mr. Y; he can be very hilarious only if you know the secret.

Wally Wordsworth

Honestly, Wally Wordsworth is not enough. Let me make another attempt to write down his name.

Name: Wally Wordsworth
Wally William Wordsworth
Wally Wallace William Wordsworth
Wally Wenger Wallace William Wordsworth
Wally Willingdon Wenger Wallace William Wordsworth
Wally Waterbury Willigdon Wenger Wallace William Wordsworth
Wally Wilkinson Waterbury Willigdon Wenger Wallace William Wordsworth

It can still go on. And this name would have run into many pages if Wally Wordsworth was the author of this book. The original Shakespearean wisdom would question what was in a name! The naming convention is just a metaphor used for describing our latest character. He had the knack of turning a 100 m sprint into a 40 Km marathon. He possessed a magical talent of endlessly elongating very simple conversations into never-ending prose.

In short, if you have to outsource an assignment of writing an epic to someone then "Quickly catch him", but if the job is to write an "Executive Summary" you must know by now, that you will have to do it yourself.

Or one can simply say that he took the word 'Wordsworth' too seriously and minced no words to prove to the world that he was indeed a Wordsworth. In short, Wally had a serious problem in keeping things short.

Wally was my colleague in office and we worked together very closely on a few projects. And yes, I am now reasonably well equipped to write a mini-thesaurus.

Special features and Tendencies

- Has mastered the art of dragging conversations and saying the same things innumerable times, in different ways.
- His SMSs are longer than emails.
- His emails are longer than short stories.
- His short stories are longer than novels.
- If he ever wrote a novel, it would be longer than River Nile.
- Ideally suited to write a thesaurus, or even a soap opera.
- He can also be a brand ambassador for an elastic making company.

Situation

I remember Wally and I were seriously pissed off with a colleague because of his laid-back attitude towards work. There are some people who come to office primarily to surf the net or make free telephone calls and spend time whaling around the coffee machine. In case you throw some work at them, they escape as if it is some deadly acid and it is their natural defense mechanism to evade it. The constant choice that these people make is between excuses and execution; if you don't want to execute it then at least think of a valid excuse. This is called the "Excuse vs. Execute" syndrome. These people have only one agenda and in corporate lingo it is called putting the ball in 'someone else's court'. After a brief session of bitching about this person, the discussion shifted to how some people only work for money. The job thus becomes purely an avenue for income generation and the matter ends there for them. There is no passion to excel or make a greater meaning out of life for such persons.

Me: I don't understand how some people work; they just want to pass the buck. These people only work for the pay cheque. I don't see passion and a sense of achievement as the driving force behind their work.

Wally: I must admit, confess and acknowledge, and also affirm that I fully agree with you. In fact, what you just said is the absolute truth. I totally second you on your thoughts and observations about some kind of co-workers. I really appreciate and am in total agreement with you on this. I must accept that I am forced to agree with you. I have no reasons or any kind of logic to defy or deny or dispute what you just said. Even at the cost of slight repetition, I can't resist saying that I fully agree with you. Work is for excellence and not for compliance.

Me(Oh god! Why did I bring up this topic?): I must leave now; something urgent to be submitted.

Wally: Please wait for some time. You have brought up a very valid and pertinent topic. It is a topic which is very relevant and holds a lot of importance. It would not be an exaggeration to say that it is one of most critical and vital factors that affects the human capital of any enterprise. All I can say is that it is one of the most significant, essential, crucial and compelling arguments for you to have put forward.

Wally went on blah, blah, blah and then he followed it up with much more blah blah.

Wally: We all come to office. We get up in the morning, have bath, read the newspaper, get ready, wear clothes, have our breakfast, have some tea or coffee and then we step out of our house. Then we all commute to office by various means like trains, buses, cars, scooters, motor cycles, taxis, auto rickshaws or some people even come walking. The entire process right from getting up in the morning to commuting to office is just a means to reach office. For some people this is just a daily chore of reaching their office and for others it is a routine way to begin the day. In this entire process, some people are mechanical, working to earn their livelihood; but there are others who enter the office with a clear agenda and an objective of making a difference. The one who wants to make a difference is the one who has passion and takes pride in what he does. He comes to give his best shot and not to earn money. Money and success definitely follows, but he is not chasing money. He is driven by something on his own, which comes from within and which is nothing but a passion to excel, it is the obsession to contribute and fervour to make a difference. All this leads to a sense of achievement, a sense of pride, a sense of fulfillment, a sense of satisfaction and most importantly, a sense of being true to our commitments.

Me (almost collapsing): Yeah, you have a point. I have to go, something really urgent.

Wally: No problem. Please carry on. We could hardly discuss this topic today. It is a very interesting topic and holds a lot of relevance. We must discuss it in detail and at length, to do justice to it.

Me: Sure. Let us a make a documentary on this topic (said with obvious sarcasm). Take care.

Wally: Why just a documentary? We must also write a book on this topic, a research paper, also write a journal, and create a website for taking pride at work. We can also form an association of likeminded professionals and works towards this goal.

It is widely believed that the entire office saw someone running frantically in the corridors and the unconfirmed reports say that it was me running from his cabin.

This talent was not just related to work related communications; he could discuss anything under the sun at length which was actually not required. If something could be aptly expressed in 17 words, Wally could spend more than 250 words to say the same thing. In today's era of T20 cricket, Wally can be compared to a 5 day Test match as far as quantitative aspect of speech is concerned.

If you ever find him: Act dumb and deaf. Just use sign language. Or at maximum, send an SMS.

CHAPTER 5 (B)

When Simon met Wally

At the time of writing this piece of fiction, Indian economy was under a bit of stress due to the aftermath of European financial crisis and a dip in Indian economy due to various economic issues. Corporate India was busy evaluating innovative methods for cost cutting and productivity management.

Being a manager and writer at the same time and using some creative liberty, I was tempted to imagine a fictitious situation where Wally Wordsworth and Simon Satellite are given a task of cost cutting and productivity management of a very large software company. Simon who does not come to the point and Wally who gets married to a point thus make an interesting study in contrast.

A hypothetical account of how I expect the interaction to unwind is produced below.

Wally: We have never met before since ours is a very large company with so many offices and employees across the globe in all the continents except Antarctica. Anyway, Antarctica does not need software engineers. However, now we are meeting with regard to a collaboration and partnership pertaining to a very crucial, critical and important project for our company.

So can you take me through the background of your experience in our company?

Simon: I like the company of my friends. Most of my friends come from affluent families and their backgrounds are very interesting. All of them work for different companies.

Wally: You seem to have missed my point. I was curious to know how our company has benefited from your contribution.

Simon: Contribution! Mahatma Gandhi made a great contribution to India; Nelson Mandela made a great contribution to South Africa and Bill Gates made a huge contribution to charity besides information technology. I forgot to mention the contribution of Mother Teresa to humanity. Contribution is a very interesting subject.

Wally: Introductions are not helping. Let me come straight to the point. This is a very major and an extremely critical responsibility handed over to us. We have to make sure that we can improve the productivity of the company, improve its effectiveness, make the margins more attractive, make the people more efficient and in some way bring about a positive impact on the bottom line and other profitability factors of the company such as profit before tax and profit after tax. At the end of it, we have to cut costs and improve the productivity.

Simon: Oh yes, I have read many books on productivity. The books on productivity are very productive. I simply love the productivity of these productive books.

Wally: Very well said, I think it cannot be said better. You have brought up a very sensitive topic of books. It is said that books are building blocks of our lives. Some people even say that a room without books is like a body without soul. I love all the books by William Shakespeare.

Simon: William Shakespeare was a very productive writer from England who wrote a lot about the Roman Empire. We must try to analyze the productivity of Roman Empire and see if we can find something interesting for our project.

Wally: Very well said! Italy is famous for its coffee. The chances are that high quality coffee beans could be responsible for their high productivity. I simply love Italian coffee whether it is cappuccino or mochaccino. I prefer to have cappuccino after dinner and mochaccino after lunch. Indian filter coffee also has its own charm, but we should not digress and come back to Italian coffee.

Simon: I am confident that we will get along very well as a team and make some fantastic recommendations for productivity improvement. Our first recommendation to the management should be as follows:

Recommendation Number 1: *After deep analysis, statistical modeling and rigorous page by page interpretation of the great works of Shakespeare; it is recommended that our company should immediately procure high quality Italian coffee machines and beans for enhancing the productivity of software engineers of our company.*

Wally: Let us take a coffee break and try to form some more meaningful, useful and sensible recommendations for the management.

The two titans met again after the coffee break to resume work on their project.

Simon: I am telling you, these coffee breaks are a big problem for productivity. Most of these software engineers go for extended coffee breaks which sometimes are longer than lunch breaks. We must devise a method to handle this problem.

Wally: Nice thought, I also feel that people are spending too much time in the toilet.

Simon: Let us make it mandatory for engineers to carry their laptops to the toilets and they can reply to their emails while seated on the pot.

Wally: This might lead to human rights violation; we have to think of an innovative and a creative way of handling this.

Simon: Let us define the maximum permissible time that can be spent in the cafeteria and the toilets. I have a suggestion; we should recommend the "Average Permissible Toilet Time" (APTT) per day and "Average Coffee Handling Time" (ACHT) per day for each employee.

Wally: The time spent on both the activities will be monitored for all the employees and Actual Toilet Time Spent (ATTS) and Actual Coffee Time Spent (ACTS) will be calculated for the entire staff on daily basis. Every evening the data will be fed into a standard computer program and MIS report will be circulated to the management.

(APTT-ATTS) or (ACHT-ACTS) should be positive for all employees, otherwise a show cause notice will be sent to the defaulting employees.

Simon: If the ATTS of any employee is abnormally high, he will have to produce a doctor's certificate to prove that he has an upset stomach. And if he brings the doctor's certificate it should be made compulsory to also get a room freshener to negate the effects of possible gas leakages from the bum tunnel.

Wally: I think it is going to be a path-breaking study on productivity management.

Our second recommendation should be as follows:

Recommendation Number 2: *To monitor the productivity of all employees a completely innovative scorecard will be printed at the end of each day which will bring about revolutionary efficiency in the toilet breaks / coffee breaks taken by our employees.*

Simon: But who will measure and monitor the actual time spent by each employee?

Wally: This is a very good, relevant and pertinent question. I feel we must hire specialists to monitor this activity. The specialists should be a top performing auditor so that this exercise is implemented effectively. These executives will be called Toilet Monitoring Officers (TMO) & Cafeteria Monitoring Officers (CMO)

Simon: This should be out third recommendation.

Recommendation No. 3: *Our management must show a visionary approach and send a directive to HRD cell to recruit 10 CMOs and 10 TMOs to implement recommendation number 2. This may seem like additional cost upfront but will have far reaching consequences on the landscape of Indian IT industry.*

Wally: With due respect to our own recommendation, I think I have reached a tipping point beyond which I will not be able to control my biological call. Before I launch a fountain in the public domain, I feel I must quickly expedite the matter in the privacy of our toilets. What do you say?

Simon: All I can say is 'come fast'. Go like Carl Lewis and come back like Usain Bolt.

I am not sure whether Wally came back like Usain Bolt. But I am sure, with these two men at the helm of affairs, there could have been many such meaningless recommendations. But the good news is that this section was pure fiction.

Goofy Gordon

Goofy Gordon was one of the top bosses in corporate India till he reached his menopause and from there started his journey of getting sacked from one job to the other till it was humanly possible for him to find a new job. The phenomenon of his sacking had almost become like monsoon rain, where you could loosely predict the approximate time when it was about to come.

- Any business being led by him was like a soccer team without a goal keeper.
- Any strategy prepared by him was like a computer without a microprocessor.

Titanic could sink right under his nose and he would not come to know about it at all. It is a borrowed expression, but suits him perfectly. The obvious problem with him was that he did have the grip on the handle, but the bigger issue was he had had no clue where the handle was.

The business review meeting for him was like playing "Spot the handle contest". He would patiently hear all department heads under him to get some idea of what was happening. If asked for an opinion, his standard response would be an "I agree" to anyone who was speaking with maximum hand and body movements. It was shocking to comprehend how a business manager could always agree with opinions voiced by sales, credit and product team at the same time.

Goofy probably understood the meaning of decision making. However, with the passage of time he had lost the flair for taking decisions. Whenever a sales person would recommend a proposal to him, Goofy would give his go ahead in a flash and "agree" with all the strengths of the case. On the same case when the credit (risk) person would highlight his opposing concerns and risks, Goofy would be the first person to be in agreement with those apprehensions. Goofy could take strong positions on both sides of the spectrum with his standard "I agree" being lent as a token of support to both the warring counterparties. With Goofy's equal agreement on sales and risk, his ability to make marginal decisions (or 'on the fence' decisions) was minimalistic. Goofy was probably a great believer in destiny. Like water, all decisions will find their own level!!

Decision-making aside, Goofy Gordon was the original inventor of *The "I Agree" Management Theory.*

If an "I agree" would not work in certain circumstances, then he would probably use the next ace, which was, "You are the head of the department and I leave this decision to you". In fact, Goofy Gordon had many dramatic variants to reflect the aforesaid point. The more graceful options that he used are mentioned below:

- Providing solutions is easy for me. But I want to change the culture; I want managers to come up with their own solutions. There is a famous Chinese proverb which says - *Give a man a fish, he will eat it for a day, but if you teach him how to fish then he will eat if for a lifetime.* I am investing for the future.

- You are the manager; you decide. Making mistakes is the stepping stone to success.

- Just imagine that I am on leave for two weeks and I have gone to the Brazilian rainforest where I am not reachable. What would you do? Take a call on your own.

- Think like an entrepreneur. Just imagine there is no boss above you and you are the last man to solve this problem. What will you do in that case?

Goofy always had intellectual theories to distribute. When you needed the fruits urgently, he would generally distribute the seeds.

Did he have a leadership style? In terms of conventional models, I don't think he would fit anywhere. However, he can be attributed to have formed a new leadership style and in simple terms his style can be summed up as *"Excessive delegation with no controls"*.

His leadership style was modelled on a concept of a utopian world which did not work in reality.

Goofy also suffered from serious concentration pangs. Very often for well-endowed women it is said, "that *they* enter the room before she does". Goofy had a different problem; he could actually leave the room while he would be physically still sitting there. Mentally, the man would be off to Phuket getting a massage and sipping his beer. This concept was fondly known to all of us as "Goofy in wonderland".

Goofy had fantastic credentials in terms of academics, having done his engineering and MBA from the most reputed institutes in India. His documentations / certifications were perfect and that's what probably kept him in good stead in finding alternative assignments after each short circuit. Goofy had about twenty years of work experience. My personal feeling is that he would have been a rockstar for the first ten years of his career. After ten years, he probably discovered more advanced technology popularly known as "Auto Pilot" Management Theory whereby he ended up knowing nothing about his work but agreeing with everyone. The advanced auto pilot style of management probably led to the fall of his reputation and his career positioning. Sometimes one loses passion after a brief success and that leads to a slow downfall of an individual. That's why from Gordon he became Goofy Gordon. As someone has said "nothing fails like success" because once you become successful you usually stop doing things that made you successful. Gordon was a victim of his own success.

This character is not just funny but also dangerous. The levels may vary but with passing success there is a risk of certain degree of menopause that gets formed in the human system.

When the thought of success enters your mind, think of Goofy Gordon and get your passion back.

Learning's from Goofy Gordon:

Goofy Gordon reinforces the need for passion and being at your best at all times. As the great Albert Einstein said:

When the Sun Rises

Every morning in Africa, When the sun rises,
A deer awakens, knowing it has to outrun the fastest Lion,
Or, be hunted to death…
But… When the sun rises,
A lion awakens, knowing it has to outrun the slowest deer,
Or, be starved to death…
It does not matter whether you are a deer or lion,
When the sun rises,
Better be running at your best.

- Albert Einstein

Fire first, aim later and pray that it hits the bull's eye

Once upon a time, an ultra exited Goofy Gordon called my colleague and me to his gigantic cabin to discuss a very big deal. Presumably, a very large MNC corporate had evinced interest in a channel finance (dealer financing in loose parlance) deal with us. The only surprising part was that the deal had originated through Goofy Gordon's contact list. To take the rituals forward, Goofy Gordon fixed our meeting and we were supposed to meet the Managing Director of the "XYZ" company.

Keeping in line with the occasion, I dressed appropriately in my newly-acquired Hugo Boss suit and struck by deadly habit of punctuality, we reached absolutely on time looking dapper , carrying some awesome-looking presentations on our laptops.

There were only two problems with this meeting that we discovered upon reaching the venue:

- One, the person we were supposed to meet was not a managing director but a *marketing director*. Obviously, he neither had the skill set nor the inclination to understand our proposal. Alternatively, Sales Director or Finance director would have also been a good choice.

- Second and the bigger problem, that he did not remember giving any such appointment. Though he had some vague but unquantifiable idea about it.

If the first problem was an injury, the second one was like rubbing salt on our wounds. Being senior managers ourselves, we felt quite callously abused by our manager.

However, the good news was that the receptionist of XYZ Company was the prettiest woman I had seen in the last 6-7 years. Besides the 'coefficient of beauty' the meeting was more disastrous than a nuclear bomb blast. The sight of this pretty woman was definitely not going to be enough to bring down our fury; we righteously bombarded into his cabin and demanded explanations on both the points once we went back to the office.

"Goofy, this is not acceptable. The guy was not the right person to be met and more importantly, he had no clue about this meeting. I value my time very much and this was very casual on your behalf to take our time and efforts for granted," I took a hard stance with my boss.

Rattled and reasonably shaken Goofy wanted to do some urgent damage control. He requested his secretary to quickly connect to this *marketing guy;* I don't remember his exact name, let's just call him Ramlal for convenience.

'Can I speak to Ramlal?'

'Speaking'.

'Hey Ramlal, Goofy on the line, how are you doing man?'

'Who Goofy'?

'Goofy ….. Goofy Gordon'.

'Who Goofy Gordon?'

Embarrassed by now, Goofy was trying to laugh the matter out.

'Ha ha ha, Goofy Gordon from "Smart Fart Company".

Goofy was laughing perpetually to maintain a false sense of cool.

'Which "Smart Fart Company?"

'Ha ha ha … Goofy Gordon ….. Smart Fart Company ……. Sky Apartments'.

'Sky Apartments, Aha,' Ramlal could remember vaguely.

'I stay on the 14th floor, remember Ramlal we met in the elevator? Goofy replied with a sigh of relief.'

'Oh yes, sorry I couldn't place you earlier,' Ramlal apologized for no fault of his.

'Ha ha ha; no problems. Remember, I discussed the channel finance idea in the elevator from the ground floor to the 14th floor and wanted my colleagues to meet you. You had just agreed when the elevator door was shutting.'

'Oh oh, someone had come, but I guess our discussion in the elevator was too casual I thought.'

'Never mind, my team will come down again.'

'Please send the proposal in writing first; I will pass it to the finance head and our sales head.'

'That's so nice of you and thanks for the anticipated help. A crisp proposal will hit your inbox very soon.' Goofy hung up.

'Sorry guys, slight communication gap.' Goofy summed up the situation.

This was the beauty cum audacity of Goofy Gordon; he could make us prepare presentations citing a contact that couldn't place him correctly till the fifth hint was given. My guess is that, it was the "fourteenth floor clue of the Sky Apartments" that finally worked.

Ramlal and Goofy Gordon stayed in the same building and had probably met once in their lifetime inside an elevator and Goofy would have forced an appointment down his throat right there.

Fishes don't need to learn swimming; it comes naturally to them; likewise 'committing blunders' was a naturally inherited trait for Goofy Gordon. The best part of Goofy Gordon was that he did similar goof ups across the hierarchy chain, ranging from a peon going right up to irking the board of directors.

The final equation looks like this:

Series of blunders = Sacking.

I am sure someday he will start his own consultancy so that no one can fire him again.

Chapter 7

Venkat Borapathy

There are several beauty pageants in the world and most of them are closely contested. There are various Grand Prix formula 1 races throughout the year and it often goes down to the wire. But if there was a competition for the most boring person on earth, our man would win by a thumping margin. He was such a big bore that even his name had oodles of boredom – Borapathy.

Most Venkatramans in the world are either referred to as Venkat or Venky; so this one was called Venkat. He is one guy who can totally put you off without uttering a single word. While there are people with names like Lakshmipathy or Ganapathy, the name Borapathy has been selected to recognize the world's greatest bore. To give you some physical perspective of things, he was short and dark, his body was perfectly cylindrical in shape. He had a thick moustache; probably with more hair than his head. His persona, his body language, his mannerism, his facial expressions, all oozed a sense of boredom. His mere presence in the room could be more tragic than a massive earthquake or a serial bomb blast. The police is popular for using third degree torture techniques while interrogating hardened criminals; Venkat can be deployed as a fourth degree torture tool by investigating agencies by simply locking the criminals along with him for a day. I am confident that the results would be astonishing. One has heard of management consultants, brand consultants; if I extend the logic further, Venkat could well be the world's first 'Torture Consultant'. I still can't resist imagining this further; I can foresee a tremendous demand for his services with many security agencies across the globe, asking him to get some truth out of the suspects. This is going to be potential demand and supply hazard; I will recommend a video conferencing initiative to be conducted by him, with each hour per day being dedicated to FBI, Scotland Yard and our own Mumbai Police. Trust me, it will work; he can be lethal even on a television, miles away from you.

His boredom was multidimensional and as the word suggests, had many elements. The description above is limited to his physical attributes, the matters got even more complicated when he opened his mouth.

Special Features and Tendencies; Venkat was the epitome of balanced boredom

- He was the brand ambassador of unsung melancholy.
- Possessed the pessimism of an eternal mourner.
- He believed that the happiness on earth submerged with the lost continent of Atlantis.
- Mistook smiling for smoking and hence considered it injurious to health.

Venkat hated everything and every possible situation in the world. I remember, India had won a very exciting cricket match (and the whole country was rejoicing) and it was a natural gesture to be celebrating after such a great win. But even in the middle of such euphoria, he was still found to be cribbing about some match which India had lost some decades back in 1987.

Like I said, he had problems with everything under the sun, so technically speaking, I can't even say that he was from Mars. I assume he was from some other galaxy and his abnormal behaviour just strengthened my belief that there could be life somewhere in the universe besides Earth. People claim to have seen the aliens; I can probably claim to have lived with an alien.

Eureka! Eureka! "Aliens do exist". It was an Archimedes moment of my life. Thank God, I had my clothes on!

He lived with us in our apartment for three months in Mumbai as we wanted a partner to share the rent. But we soon realized that saving money is not always the most important thing and Venkat was instrumental in teaching us this important lesson. Of course he moved out of the apartment in three months. Needless to say we celebrated that day like it was Christmas.

There is no major scientific discovery in stating that human beings are only living organisms capable of smiling and laughing. Despite this, it was my dream to see a mild smile on his face at least once in my lifetime. In fact, I never even wanted to see him smiling profusely or laughing loudly; that would be too unfair to expect and could have disturbed the biological balance of his body. It was surprising to observe how one could live all his life with one stupid consistent expression. Normal human beings automatically tend to modulate their voice as they speak different things, reflecting different moods and emotions. Venkat was an exception here too, having maintained a monotone for the last 28 years. (I lost touch with him after that and thankfully so.)

He was a topic of research for me at one point of time as to how someone can dislike everything so much; it was always very interesting to probe him with different questions to which an average human being would have multiple answers.

'Which is your favorite movie?'

'All movies are stupid; a total waste of time.'

'But I am sure you must have liked at least one.'

'There is not even a single sensible movie ever made in the world.'

'What about television?'

'Television is called an idiot box, why should I watch it?'

His answers were actually like an old man who was royally frustrated with life and has only bitterness and a few countable years left to live. This led to creation of a path breaking theory called the "T + 50 Theory".

This theory emphasizes that a few persons are actually mentally much older than their physical age and this was probably the root cause of their phenomenal boredom.

T being the physical age and 50 years being the boredom drag attached to it. Venkat was 28 years, therefore his final mental score after applying this theory was (28+50) = 78 years.

What more could you expect from a 78 year old man?

If you apply this theory across the people you meet, you will be able to comprehend their situation better and deal with them with more patience.

This theory comes with a floating variable factor, which means you can modify the variable as T+25 Theory or T+15

Theory from person to person. Everyone can't be as boring as Venkat to deserve a "T+50" tag. So next time you meet a torture king or a big bore, identify the variable factor.

After the discovery of this theory, I became rather considerate to his replies.

Me: 'I am going to have a burger, are you coming?'

Venkat: 'Burger!! Bloody junk food, not good for intestines.'

Me: 'Yeah, you are right. I think you must have oats for dinner.'

Me: 'Venkat, whisky?' *(How could I dare to ask this in the first place?)*

Venkat: 'Whisky is not good for the liver.'

Me: 'I think liquor should get banned.'

Me: 'Are you coming for the night show of the latest movie?'

Venkat: 'No night show for me, I have to go to office. Early to bed, early to rise makes a man healthy, wealthy and wise.'

Me: 'I agree, you must sleep soon, anyways this movie would come on television after one or two years, you can watch it then.'

We were not unemployed either and probably had a more progressive career than him, but it didn't seem to matter any longer, as I had realized that he was about to turn 79 next week and was right in his own way. T+50 Theory became a tool for accepting his behaviour.

Venkat just did not seem to enjoy anything in life (I am saying this at the cost of repetition). He would keep sitting idly somewhere in the apartment, just doing nothing. This led to another theory called as the "The State of Nothingness Theory", a state almost permanent for him.

Nearly three months passed in observing his ridiculous tendencies and framing new theories from time to time. The strange turn of events took place towards the last week of his stay in our apartment which led to total antithesis of what has been described so far. It so happened, that Venkat won some incentive scheme in his office and was nominated for a Bangkok trip. One of our other room partners, Martin was his colleague (it was his referral that actually got him the place in our apartment and he was never pardoned for such a rotten referral) and incidentally he also won a trip for himself.

Their return from Bangkok was a personally satisfying and eye opening moment for me. Before you get wrong ideas, I personally did not go to Bangkok. It was Martin who described a few incidents about how Venkat went wild in a topless bar in Bangkok. He was found smiling, laughing and getting explicitly naughty.

Martin did the first smart thing in his life by capturing these wild moments on a camera with Venkat beaming, laughing and going totally out of control.

Venkat even went on to spend some personal and private moments with the bar girl who drove him nuts. The details of those private moments are not known to us, but we have the creative license to imagine what a 79 year old man would have done.

The girl was named Christine and she was no ordinary Christine, as she fulfilled our dream to see this man happy. 'This christine could actually melt a rock.'

The boring Venkat finally laughed and even got naughty; a woman can do miracles.

But the fact remains, he is the most boring person on earth, albeit some 'Christine Moments' for temporary relief.

> **If you ever find him:** Just close your eyes and shut your ears.

CHAPTER 8

Miss Chutney Spears

A country with a population of more than 1 billion is always expected to have its share of problems. Although India is one of the countries where adoption of English as language has been phenomenally good, it is also substantiated by mushrooming of call centers in the recent past. Despite this, English is still a bit of a struggle for certain sections of society.

My career has been majorly involved in dealing with large corporate in a B2B environment; while in between I had a very short stint in retail space. One of the most hilarious memories of this retail stint pertains to a random job application that I received through an email. The application originated from the roots of Punjab which is considered the food bowl of India. The emails were grammatically, aesthetically and logically demented. To make matters worse, even the spellings were absolutely innovative and would send a linguistic scholar into a state of paralysis.

The emails from the applicant are reconstructed below to the best of my memory. I still feel that my version is far classier as I cannot possibly match the applicant's talent to rape the

English language and also to go completely off the tangent for simplest of queries.

From: Chutney Spears

Sub: Job apply

The Manager of the charge

I is Chutney Spears. I am belongs to Sandhwan Tehsil & District - Faridkot. I am M.A. Punjabi and others qualification Punjabi and English Stenography, Computer in one year Diploma course, Punjabi Stenography Instructor Course. I am a volunteer in Red Cross short stay home Faridkot close by and I am also work in computer typing. She is very serious. She work is very honestly. She is very hard worker. My hobby is working to continue. I am a good girl. My project location is Faridkot. My mother was expired. She was very nice ladies. She was loves me. My father was a farmer. He is very nice persons. I am four brother and one sisters. The sister is I only, i.e. I am my own sister.

I am want the job. Please give it to Chutney. She is very need it.

Yours forever,

Chutney Spears

Though I could feel some amount of empathy for the applicant and could understand the struggle she might be going through, but I found the email too funny and cute. The best part of the email was this constant switch she made between addressing herself as I and sometimes as she. I was young and fairly inexperienced, hence could not resist the temptation of replying to her anticipating another gem of a mail in return.

From: Jas Anand
Re: Job Apply
Dear Ms. Chutney Spears,
Thank you for sending your application. We would like to know more about your competences, areas of strength and details of institutions from where you have completed your education. Kindly also clarify for which post you have sent the application.

Regards,
Manager in Charge
Smart Fart Company

From: Chutney Spears
Re: Re : Job Apply
I is Chutney Spears again. I am still belongs to Sandhwan tehsil, Faridkot district. Very much thank you for your reply to my apply.

Happiness feeling all over me as job is importance to her. I am very competence persons. My main competence is my cooking. My food cooking is best in my villages. My chicken curry are very nice, tasty and delicious. My father and my 4 brothers are like very much my chicken biryani also. The Chutney I make with food is best inside entire Punjab, hence nicknamed is me as 'Chutney'.

Myself is also very good in cleaning and dusting of my father houses. I am very sportsman person. She was throwing discus throw in college and schools. She was also throwing javelin throw. Chutney is very strong person. You want to know area of strengths; I have very strong shoulders and muscles.

My education was from educative institute.

I am not able to understanding the question of post. I did not apply through post, I am apply through email.

She wants the job to get her only. Please confirm fast

Regards,

Chutney

I was tempted like hell to continue the replying saga. But alas, work ethics did not permit this. More than work ethics, it was also the sin of giving someone a false hope. We were not a restaurant nor a sports company and neither a housekeeping services company. Being in financial services, I had to let this one go.

Section 2

Matters of the Heart

Larry Love

Ambition and desire can make people do unbelievable things. The obsession with your dream can create untiring and relentless energy to pursue goals till they are accomplished. Men have often dreamt of scaling new heights, including literally climbing the Mount Everest or going even higher up to the moon and beyond that as well. It is often said "Money has no color", it is true about ambition too. I have never been able to comprehend how each of us can get obsessed with a particular thought.

In general, Larry Love is a great guy in all respects. His ambition was not Himalayan or ambitious by any standard. On the contrary, it was the most basic need in life which could be captured in four main points as follows:

1. To find a perfect (10/10) girl of his dreams
2. Followed by madly falling in love with her
3. Hoping she loves him too
4. Happy ending

Point number 1 is strictly a matter of demand and supply. The demand for such women across the species called man is very high and unfortunately the supply side has its own limitations. (The same applies to man without gender bias.)

Point number 2 was the easiest proposition of the four point agenda, so I will not spend much time on it. Point 2 would happen automatically whenever he came across a 10/10.

Point number 3 was the gigantic bottleneck and this is where most of his dreams turned to nightmares. I can recall endless conversations with him over a glass of beer analyzing why his candidature is not regarded seriously by women in question.

Unfortunately, point number 4 was totally dependent on point number 3.

To me, he was an "Eternal Romeo without his Juliet". I was his close confidant and advisor (for whatever little I was worth, especially in these love matters) in shaping up the strategies for fulfilling his dream.

Larry is a cute looking, slightly plump, fair and tall, well mannered, well dressed and a reasonably good conversationalist with promising career prospects. It was baffling that a guy with such credentials was finding no takers in the market. It would have been a tough case for management consultants to crack, because if they did any SWOT (Strengths, weakness, opportunities and threats) analysis or made attractiveness matrix, he would fare well, at least on paper.

But the reality on ground was different; he was still single and always ready to mingle.

Little did he imagine that he would face so many challenges before realizing his dream. For the first time after college, Larry fell madly in love with a fantastic woman, very well knowing that she was married and also knowing that she was not particularly interested in any romantic alliance with him. They were good friends and I guess that was the ideal level to maintain. Love has its own rules and often chooses to follow no rules; very soon he had crossed the first two stages of his 4 point agenda. The lady was not interested in his extracurricular activities. Reality dawned and so did good sense and Larry moved on.

A few months passed, Larry got friendly with a girl called Maria. Before he could realize, our man was already in love with her. Maria was a mind-blowing woman, she had already blown away someone's heart a few years ago and was planning to get married to him. Maria already had her Martin in place, leaving no vacancy for Larry yet again.

As a rule, each heartbreak was followed by 'Our Long Beer Sessions" which could run on for a whole week after office hours, those could well, have been branded as a "heartbreak weeks".

But Larry was very different from all of us, he had two distinct strengths:

1. He could overcome heartbreak very fast. Over a period of time, a heartbreak for him became equivalent to India losing a cricket match – a bit of frustration followed by a hope to win the next one.

2. He could very quickly find another woman to fall in love with.

During his struggle period, I had actually framed a theory for him called the "Prospective Wife Theory". There was a period in his life when he used to look upon every woman he came across as a prospective wife and later eliminated for different reasons such as:

- "Already Married"
- "Does not meet the requirements"
- "Existing Boyfriend"
- "Tried very hard, but bad luck yet again"

Larry was desperate to find love and get married. The pressure from his parents to settle for the classic Indian arranged marriage was very high and it was adding to his urgency of falling in love. Despite an active implementation of the "Prospective Wife Theory", the results seemed to be missing. Students of physics are taught the difference between "Distance" and "Displacement". For me, his situation was a practical metaphor of this concept, where he was covering a huge amount of distance in terms of efforts without a single inch of displacement.

Bottom line, he was still without love.

The situation demanded urgent brainstorming, and we met again duly supported by cans of beer and some crispy tandoori chicken. Without any scientific and biological validation, to me beer is a source of Vitamin B and chicken a source of Vitamin C. Larry of course, very badly needed Vitamin L in the form of love.

People very often talk about their first crushes; but Larry could talk about his 37th crush with equal intensity.

Larry re-considered his 4 point agenda. He identified point number 1 as the biggest reason for failure. The root cause was that 10/10 girls are either hooked or already married. He lowered the criteria to 8 / 10 instead and re-launched himself in the market. With lowering of the criteria, the target market had visibly expanded, a database of 7 prospects which could have been targeted as girlfriends was created. In sales management lingo, this exercise can be referred as "Funneling the prospects".

The revised strategy did work for him and he finally found some companionship after some years of famine. Actually, he was just flirting around this time. But still it worked well for him. Any place struck with drought needs rain in the first place. In fact, Larry got involved in two timing at the same time. The two flirtatious affairs actually toned him down from being "Highly Frustrated in Search of Love" to "Still looking for real love".

Larry sleepwalked through his flings here and there, till he finally met another 10/10 and this time around, his luck was 10/10 too.

Things finally clicked for him at last and he is now a happily married man. His wife is not aware of his earlier tendencies and the "prospective wife theory"; this book might just change the impression.

Relax Larry; all the names in this book are changed to protect identities.

> **If you ever find him**: Keep your sisters away from him. He intends no harm but can fall in love. Avoid complications; keep a distance.

Matters of the Heart – Part 2

A man in love or – rather a man in the process of "falling in love" – lives life with an altogether different fervor. Such a man always finds trees greener than normal, water bluer than usual and probably can even find a crow more graceful than a duck.

The topic of love reminds me of three interesting anecdotes; one of which obviously pertains to Larry Love and the other two are related to me but are clearly inspired by 'matters of the heart' patented by Larry:

1. What's in an address?
2. Cardamom Kiss
3. Love Pentagon

CHAPTER 9 (B)

What's in an address?

Larry and I were part of the same department in our organization. As per the process of new product roll out, we were scheduled to travel together to Delhi for training our business associates and channel partners. Delhi has many beautiful facets and one of them is the beautiful faces you can see. Please don't get my intentions wrong, but also don't forget I am travelling with Larry who is forever in search of his "Miss 10/10" with his "Prospective wife theory" activated.

It so happened that among the twenty-five participants of the training program that we were conducting, one turned out to be a stunningly beautiful girl. While one can see perfect beauties like Aishwarya Rai in Hindi films or Angelina Jolie in Hollywood films, the girl I am talking about is probably the best you can see in real life. In the colloquial context I can rephrase or re-describe her as "Aishwarya Rai" or "Angelina Jolie" of day to day living.

It did not hold any specific importance for me. The only relevance for me can be best explained through a metaphor that an air conditioned room is always more preferable to a normal sultry room. It was just an added advantage to be chilled up by her presence. However, at the back of my mind I was confident that Larry's prospective wife theory must be in play and he might be contemplating whether to go for honeymoon in Maldives or Mauritius. For the rest of us, it was just a hygiene factor but for Larry, wedding bells were at stake.

Well, the first session of the training got over and we broke for lunch. Incidentally and accidently, this girl (For convenience let us call her Lucy, because I don't remember her name) and one more gentleman joined us for lunch at our table. There is nothing more to read between the lines; normally I have seen that trainers / key session speakers get some extra kind attention that comes attached with "big brotherly" feelings. There was really nothing to read between the lines; but please don't forget we also have Larry in the picture. And you all know by now that "Prospective wife theory" is working at its rampant best. After a few nonsensical discussions pertaining to the product, the conversations shifted to general things.

"So Larry, where do you stay in Mumbai?" she asked (Lucy was a frequent visitor to Mumbai).

"I stay at Nallasopara," Larry replied

Nallasopara is a distant suburb of Mumbai, which was fairly less known at the point of time when this episode occurred; about ten years ago. The sound of Nallasopara is not honey to the ears either.

She gave an indifferent look and a not happy response for some reason. Larry of course did not like it and for some reason, I could not miss catching her not so pleasant response.

Then she happened to ask me the same question. I was actually staying at 7 Bungalows which is definitely a buzzing suburb in Mumbai which may be about three kilometres from a very popular locality called Juhu. I had taken deep cognizance of her response and to give her a broad perspective of things, I generally happened to reply, "I stay in Juhu". (In a city which has an end to end stretch of about 60 kilometres; 3 kilometres is just 5% in magnitude, so it was not a blatant lie but a minor deviation from truth in my opinion. Please don't forget there was a real life Angelina Jolie sitting in front of me and any man would have some feeble tendencies to put across impressive data points.)

"Oh, I Love Juhu. One of my uncles stays there. It is a very nice place to stay," she replied.

"Of course, it is a great place to stay," I replied.

"Somehow I have never heard about Nallasopara," she continued (this was not required, she did not stay in White House either).

"So do you go for a jog to the beach?" she asked me another question.

"At least five times a week," I lied without blinking an eye. I still don't know why I lied.

"I love walks on the beach or by the hill side," she added.

"I am originally from Dehradun and my parents still live there. I have had the best of hills and beaches," I just summed up the matter.

"Lucky you!" Lucy sealed the discussion.

Larry was quiet and sulking. He did not like me discussing Juhu, beaches and hills with his prospective wife. It was viewed by him as trespassing into his estate without prior permission. If murders were permitted legally, I would have been dead by now.

The lunch got over and by evening the entire training was over. But I knew in my heart of heart that the episode was not yet over for Larry. It did not really matter to her where we stayed. It was a very casual discussion. But for Larry, nothing is casual when it pertains to falling in love. He did not say a word but the entire day he gave me that passive feeling that I stole his thunder in front of a virtuous girl. Anyway, the matter was dead and buried.

Many months passed, the Juicy Lucy was forgotten and never even discussed. One evening after office, Larry and I decided to stop by at my house for a couple of drinks.

I stopped a cabbie and asked him "7 Bungalows?"

Spontaneously Larry chipped in, "Oh! Now you remember 7 Bungalows; why didn't you tell him Juhu?"

I was shocked to hear this and it transported me back to the lunch table discussion with Lucy. Although several months had passed, Larry had still not forgotten the lunch episode and messed up plans for his honeymoon.

If Shakespeare was alive, he could have contemplated "What's in an address?"

Chapter 9 (C)

Cardamom Kiss

Fist for a fist, stare for a stare, I can match it all, in most cases, but she is an exception. I go weak in my knees when she smiles at me. I always tried very hard to resist, but she somehow managed to drive me crazy. Sheena was a friend. I wish that was all, but the fact was that I had a major crush on her - head over heel type.

Sheena was a good friend, probably the only girl in my life with whom I used to enjoy having coffee and conversations. She was a completely adorable person with great versatility in different aspects of life and it was evident that she was fond of me too. With passing days, I was getting hooked on to her and the problem with me was that I was getting too impatient to cross this phase of friendship and attach a deeper meaning to this relationship.

I often thought of telling her my true feelings, but words rather guts desert me at the opportune time. Guys shouldn't behave like this but what to do, it was my first experience of love, perhaps my first infatuation. It was getting difficult for me to keep this secret. I had to somehow tell someone. Who can be better than Sheena? After a few days of in-depth analysis, some complex calculations and intense decision-making, I decided to tell her the truth – my feelings for her. The mission was aptly titled "Debut Disclosure". At this stage a couple of my friends from the neighborhood were roped in for successful implementation of the project. Raj was appointed as a project executive; his highness Jimmy was the project manager, the man who would steer my ship to the coast.

Raj was a fair, tiny fellow, funny in more aspects than one. If a normal person can utter about hundred words in a minute under standard circumstances, Raj could manage a hundred and fifty. He stood 62 inches above the mean sea level, if at all he stood straight. He could have looked clean, if at all he made an attempt.

Raj was inducted in the project for "psychological reasons". His key responsibility was to motivate me. Raj always gave me a superiority complex; he always did a world of good to my confidence. I always felt smarter than him. Hope you have understood the "psychological reason". On the positive side, I must admit that he had a good sense of humour. Jimmy on the other hand was a smart, fair six feet chap and a year senior to me. Jimmy had an envious track record with a string of girlfriends. Jimmy was my strategist, my coach and of course my project manager.

The mission was flagged off on January 17, 1994. The project manager had fixed the completion date as February 14, 1994 when I was supposed to formally announce my love to her and it was tactically selected keeping in view Valentine's Day.

"The D – Day is too soon," I resisted.

"No, 28 days are enough."

"You already know her very well. Time, tide and girls wait for no man," said Jimmy

This was lesson number one. Wow. "Time, tide and girls wait for no man".

Prof. Jimmy Kalra started the course and the first part was "General Introduction to the Eve's world". I religiously took down the notes; it was more important than my mathematics lecture. Raj was a camouflaged student too, anticipating a similar situation for himself in the future.

Section I of course dealt with sensibilities, behaviour and globally accepted likes and dislikes of girls. Jimmy used modern teaching techniques like group discussion and debates to get his point across.

The group discussion on "why women mature faster than men" gave me important insights into their psychological construct. I was also taught the interpretation of their body language. This session took about three days. Jimmy was the teacher and Raj took the viva. I cleared the first section to their satisfaction.

At the end of section I, Jimmy gave me a flash card with 8 important tips:

- Be a good listener when a girl speaks.
- Give her that extra super special attention, more than any other man can give.
- Don't offer solutions to her problems impulsively. First understand them.
- Be gentle and polite.
- Women are at par with men. Respect their independence.
- Be honest. Honesty is a more precious commodity than crude oil in this age.

- If at all you compromise, do not let it reflect on your face.
- Finally, use your sense of humour to the best effect.

Raj ensured that I understood the practical implications of these golden rules.

I was ready to go on to Section II of the course, which was referred as "Wooing the Lady". This phase dealt with the mannerism and behaviour which make you score the brownie points with the women.

Section III was the "art of proposing" by creating a conducive setting for expression of love. The entire syllabus containing the 3 sections was finished in 7 days. The effort was concentrated towards converting my status from a good friend to a boy friend.

"This is a very important phase of the whole process."

"You have to implement all that you have learnt in your course in the next 21 days."

"Yupp."

"Be cool, act cool. Forget for sometime that you love her. Be normal in front of her and simply woo her."

"Treat her like a lady. Treat her like a queen."

"Give her that extra attention, more than any other guy. Blend chivalry with coolness, right behaviour at the right time."

"And I think it's time to take her out on a date."

"Provided she agrees," I uttered.

"Where will you take her?"

"For a movie."

"Which one?"

"*Dirty Dancing* is quite an attraction these days."

"Forget is, she may flip for Patrick Swayze – movie is a bad idea."

"You better take her to Mussourie."

"It has all ingredients of a good date – long drive, lovely mountains, beautiful scenery and it will give you enough time for developing that extra emotional intimacy."

"But what if she says no?" I was still a pessimistic seeker.

"Shut up and be positive."

"When and where will you ask her?"

"After the physics tuitions, this evening."

"All the best," replied Jimmy.

"Thanks mate."

I wore the new Armani shirt my cousin had bought from London and went for the Physics tuition. Actually my dressing sense had improved after falling in love and the best part is that she had acknowledged this.

"I hope she comes today," I thought to myself and there she was dressed in a pink suit looking like a rose bud. Sheena was smart, beautiful, rather very beautiful, Punjabi girl. "Big black eyes, lovely long hair, fair complexion, razor sharp features and tons of style". If I were given a choice of writing an essay on Taj Mahal or Sheena, I would prefer the latter any time.

Opposite poles attract each other; Physics is just too accurate. I hope this Physics turns into a positive Chemistry between us. I was least bothered what Prof. Bawa was teaching; I was busy rehearsing my lines to be spoken after the class. The class was not eternal and got over in time; suddenly I could feel a sense of anxiety in my body.

"Hi!"

"Hey Sheena!"

"You are looking very pretty, prettier than ever before."

"Shut up," she said mischievously.

"Why? You don't like compliments."

"How many girls do you compliment everyday?"

"Once in a decade, when I come across someone like you." I said.

She seemed pleased.

"There was heavy snowfall in Mussoorie yesterday, three inches deep on the mall road," I paved way for myself.

"I know."

"Don't you think it is better to be in Mussoorie, than attending this stupid Physics tuition in Dehradun."

"Let's plan out sometime, let us check with Ronnie, Richa, Chotu and company, if they are game for Mussorrie," she said after some thought.

"There are enough tourists in Mussorrie, why do you want it to be more crowded?... Can't just the two of us go?"

There was no response; she just kept staring at the road ahead, so I added, "I am sure, I am not that boring. And not that dangerous too."

"Let me think."

"Okay, so what have you thought?"

"I need time, a day or two."

"Till then the snow will melt, and it will weep off faster if you say no."

"Okay, how and when do you propose to take me to Mussoorie?"

"I have a dad, and dad has a car and that answers the first part of your question. Tomorrow is a Sunday and we need not even miss the Physics tuition."

"Where will you pick me up?'

"You meet me at Chick Chocolate, at 10.00 am."

"No, you pick me up from my house," came the words I had been waiting for.

"As you wish, meeting your father is always a delight."

Though in reality, even the thought of Major General Sabharwal (her father to be precise) made me nervous and much disoriented. He was in charge of thousands of army men in Dehradun and had developed a false notion that he was primarily responsible for every citizen in Dehradun. He was a tough cookie and self appointed revolutionary. But the best part of Sheena was that he she was absolutely unbothered with the hoop and hoopla surrounding her father.

Anything for love, I thought.

"Bye, see you tomorrow at 10.00."

A walk in the clouds with Sheena was definitely an exciting idea. Jimmy and Raj were happy to know about the developments. Life is nothing but meeting challenges, one after the other. After extracting a 'yes' from Sheena for the Mussoorie trip, I was left with the daunting task of borrowing the car from my father and some money too. My age of 18 and the absence of a valid driving license were the factors I had to fight.

"Dad, I have something very important and urgent to discuss with you."

"What is it?" (With a stern expression, smelling a rat.)

"I need your car for a day and that's not all, I need some Indian currency notes, about Rs. 500/-."

"Car and Rs. 500, /- now that cannot be a coincidence. Why do you need the two together?" he asked with a fatherly suspicion.

"My friends are asking for a treat and we are planning to go to Mussoorie."

"You know my age?"

"You are quite secretive about it, but your I-Card says 50."

"So you know I am 50 and you know a little arithmetics too."

"Sorry, couldn't figure out your comment."

"A person, who is 50, has definitely crossed the age of 18."

"Oh, that's a valid point."

"So why don't you tell me the real reason. Name the girl you want to take out on a date."

"Dad, you are a genius...Her name is Sheena."

"She is too good for an idiot like you."

"Yeah, but I am a firm believer in Einstein."

"What has Einstein got to do with it?" asked my confused dad, a commerce student.

"The great Einstein had brilliantly articulated that 'Genius is 99% perspiration and 1% inspiration."

"But why don't you perspire for the right cause?" he said with fatherly concern.

"Can you be a little more specific and direct? Do you want me to start a welfare foundation or an NGO at the age of 18?"

"I am talking about your studies. Your books are lying virgin, why don't you go and read them."

"Dad, I have always been a good student."

"And if you have the false impression about being a good student then I must correct that. You had just quoted Thomas

Edison and not Albert Einstein," he exercised his knowledge and fatherly authority, together.

"Okay. Chill out for a day but mind you, I shall not entertain such requests again."

He also gave me seven hundred rupees, which was a generous amount in those days. I stood in front of my father and delivered a very emotional speech on 'his greatness and benevolence' and he was highly moved by my performance.

It was time to work out the nitty-gritties. I prepared a blueprint for the plan of action along with Jimmy and Raj. It was the most anxious night of my life. I got up at seven, my mother was rather surprised but she was soon apprised of the situation. She insisted on making sandwiches for the way. Motherly sandwiches appeared very unromantic and I rejected the offer. She came up with some more culinary ideas and I politely turned all of them down.

I rushed off to Ellora's Bakery, picked up a Black Forest cake and reached Sheena's house at ten. I picked her up very cleverly, avoiding the Major General.

Someoneelse'sdaughterinsomeoneelse'scar,lifecangetpretty interesting at times. I knew the importance of today, historians will be observing this day with curiosity. It was my best opportunity to charm her. Will there be a *Romeo and Juliet* Version 2.0?

Time will tell.

"So, Sheena, welcome to the joy ride," and presented her a yellow rose.

"Hope so," and "thanks for the rose."

"Nice shirt, Jas. I like your choice of late."

"You are my choice too." (I said to myself)

It was Jimmy's shirt, but I was quick to acknowledge the compliment with a firm and smiling thank you.

Mussoorie is about 27 kilometre from Sheena's house in Dehradun. I had taken 27 roses with me, one to be given after each kilometer.

"Sheena, one more rose."

"You gave me one."

"I wish I could give you the entire rose garden."

"Enough, stop getting melodramatic. Stop watching these Hindi films."

Most consumers are familiar with concept of EMIs, payable to a financial institution against the loan taken by them. To me her love was an asset, for which I was more than willing to an EMI of 1 rose per kilometre and that too in advance.

It was after 14 EMIs that we reached halfway to Mussoorie, where there are a few Machans often used by the travellers to take a break and have a good look at the awesome scenery with long unwinding roads. I removed the black forest cake and asked her to cut it. She found the idea pretty stupid but she did cut the cake gently with her soft hands.

I loved everything about her, including her style of cutting the cake. To me it was a 'Picture Perfect' moment, with Sheena besides me on the Machan and we being surrounded by the magnanimous Shivalik mountain range (the lower Himalayas). Besides the beauty and charm of Sheena, it was mountains which mattered a lot to me, something obvious for anyone growing in such a beautiful valley.

The mountain ranges have a unique charm and depth associated with them; as you keep climbing the elevation, you can see the next set of mountain ranges, perfectly showcasing the layers of enormity that nature has in store for us. Sheena too had many layers and her sheer range was one of the most magnetic aspects of her personality. From her appearance, she was an urban, hip, cool, classy, street smart and an ultra gorgeous girl. The layer beneath that contained an intelligent, well-read, determined, hardworking and a focused individual who could talk on philosophy, sports, movies, politics, religion and academics with equal ease. She was unbelievably whacky, humorous and witty with the people she was comfortable with and also exuded unique warmth which makes any woman absolutely irresistible. Sheena was like an amalgamation of different forms of human goodness rolled into one incomparable person. The discovery process was still on and I was sure that I would find many more layers with the passage of time.

We took off for Mussoorie after a brief break on the Machan and after repaying 13 more EMIs, we finally reached our destination. It seemed like a perfect day, with the clouds hustling across the Mall Road lending moisture to the air. I felt like a cloud myself, waiting to pour my feelings on her. It could well have been a cloudburst if I ever told her what she really meant to me.

Jimmy had strictly warned me not to say any such thing on this trip, he believed in waiting for the opportune time. He was probably a seasoned player in this game, but for me it was not about playing to a plan. The more time I spent with her, I realized it was the innocence of my attraction which was the purest part of this relationship.

While walking on the Mall Road, I understood that it was about Sheena and me, and I don't need any advice from anyone. I was beginning to cherish the moments I was spending with her, and the project "debut disclosure" was becoming meaningless. Though Jimmy was a well wisher, I decided to dump his section 1, 2 and 3 right there. Like water, my love will find its way, I was sure.

We dropped by at an Italian restaurant for lunch as the Princess of Dehradun expressed the desire to have a pizza. I was pretty much a pizza hater, but for me it was a moment of truth, I had never enjoyed pizza so much in my life before. Love is a catalyst which can turn dislikes into simple pleasures of life.

"People matter, pizzas don't". It was a big lesson for me that day as I realized that "unfulfilled desires" or "desires in process" have great power to transform.

"I love Italian food – pizzas, risottos and cartinis," she said

I was totally in love with everything she loved, and developed an instant infatuation for Italy. From Roman architecture to the soccer great Roberto Baggio to racing car brand Ferrari and the gondolas of Venice, Italy was all over my mind. I was about to plan our honeymoon starting from Rome going down to Sicily, but she interrupted me.

"Why did you give me yellow roses?"

"I thought whites are too boring and reds could be too daring."

"Your problem is you think too much, just cut the threads and stop attaching reason for everything. Roses are red, that's the way it should be. But I liked the idea that you carried 27 of them."

"Those who associated red roses with love are silly, love actually has no colour and you can't take shelter in a colour of a flower to express your feelings," she went on.

"Roses seem like your favorite topic, why don't you tell me

more about the petals, corollas and the pollen grains?"

"Stop making fun of me," she nudged me with her elbow.

'How about starting a horticulture business. The hills are anyway conducive for growing flowers. Our brand would be "Roses R Red" and I would ban any other color besides red." I persisted on pulling her leg

She tapped me on my cheek, "Stop it now, will you?"

A tap on my cheek, a nudge from her elbow, and pat on my shoulder – these small expressions gave me immense sense of joy. I have always placed a lot of importance to these small gestures. Relationships are all about the comfort level and these were important signs.

"Tell me one thing you dislike about me," she asked me

"You are like a Tsunami, someone I can't resist."

"Hey, I can't be that destructive."

"Ask me, I have been washed away."

"Can't you tell me seriously what you dislike about me?"

"You are like cocaine, so addictive."

"Forget it, you wont tell."

"People usually ask what you like about me? How come you come up with such anti questions? Ask me what I like in you and I can keep speaking till morning."

"But I know what you like about me."

"How do you know?"

"I can read minds. Just joking, but if I didn't know that, I wouldn't be here in Mussoorie with you," she cut me short

"Ok, tell me what do you like in me?"

"Your positive energy and your genuineness, you are subtle in your expressions and your sense of humour."

"Time to go back, before it gets too late," she said.

"Right away!" I excused myself to get the car.

Never give 27 roses to anyone, it had better be 54. And the next 27 better be the reddest ever possible. I picked up the roses before getting the car and the ritual continued every kilometre till I dropped her to her house.

"You are mad."

"Mad about you."

"Bye, take care," she ruffled my hair.

I nearly fainted with her touch and didn't touch my hair the entire night. Sheena was confident and very comfortable with her expressions. I liked her sense of spontaneity and ability to be in control of things. You won't find many girls like her; she was probably amongst the 'Limited Edition' of women created by God.

You can well imagine my infatuation with her.

Jimmy and Raj came running to my house as soon as I reached. I was pretty muted about the whole thing. They probably thought it hadn't worked out well, but what they thought didn't matter to me anymore. They were great friends and well wishers, but I was too much in love to make my private moments with her a group discussion anymore. This was the 'moment of truth' for me; the moment I realized that Sheena mattered more than anyone else. The whole episode started on a frivolous note with Jimmy and his tricks, but thankfully was now being dealt with utmost honesty and free flowing emotions.

She met me the next day at tuitions again.

"Yesterday was good fun," she said

"Yesterday once more?" I said.

"Sure, but the treat is on me this time. How about a movie next Saturday?"

"Whatever you say."

The week passed, meeting at the physics tuitions and spending some more time after that. The Saturday date went as per schedule. Though the movie was ridiculous, the time spent with her was precious. And equally precious were the packets of popcorn and bottle of Pepsi shared with her.

"Horrible movie," she said.

"I think it was great," I said.

"Are you mad?"

"I mean spending time with you was great. Who would care about the movie, especially when sitting next to you for three hours!"

"Oh really! Even a lifetime would not be enough, right?" she said with a twinkle in her eyes.

"Yeah, that's right. How did you guess my exact sentiments Miss Sheena Sabharwal?"

"Because you are the king of melodrama. Now stop flirting and drop me home in the next ten minutes."

In precisely nine and half minutes, I dropped her at her house.

"We still have 30 seconds to say good bye."

"Good bye, good boy."

Our closeness grew, and we started spending more time together after tuitions, eating a lot of junk food together, shopping together, lots of movies and even had another trip to Mussoorie. It was not just about spending fun time together; we started exchanging study notes as the examinations were nearing. In this process, I discovered that she was very methodical in her studies and she would have discovered how horrible my handwriting was.

"Your handwriting really sucks," she had specially called me up to say this.

"I know, that's one reason why I have still not written you a love letter."

"There you start again; can't you be serious?"

"I am damn serious; I will type one instead of writing with my own hand, as soon as the exams get over."

"Huh, now focus on exams and just a tip, typing a love letter is a bad idea and typing for me is an even worse one," she said mischievously.

"Don't worry, I will write it to Sharon Stone."

"Sure, try your luck; bye now. I will call you If I get stuck somewhere in Algebra."

Valentine's Day came and went away; I couldn't say a word, neither did she. But yes, we went for an early dinner that day. I realized that the D-Day had lost its relevance and I started enjoying the process of discovering her. Relationships are all about this process of exploring each other and that is the most magnetic part of falling in love.

Life was cruising along very well with balanced doses of studies, Sheena and satisfaction. I was completely at ease with her and was sure she liked me, or perhaps even loved me. Love is nothing but being happy together and not needing any third person; by this definition, we were mutually in love. On a few evenings spent together, the thought did come to me that I must now disclose my feelings to her, but it is strange that on your first such experience, the words get stuck in your throat and do not come out at all.

"I will surely tell her the next day," I kept thinking, but that also didn't seem to work at all in my case.

On one of the evenings, we went for coffee near the hill side, I wanted to tell her how much I loved her. She was her chirpy self and kept talking about various things. I was just not able to concentrate on what she was saying. While walking with her, I was trying to evaluate whether it would be more effective to say a direct "I am madly in love with you" or an indirect expression like "You have driven me mad, I think of you all the time". Despite the thorough evaluation, I still could not muster the courage to tell her the truth.

We were walking past some towering trees and I was still trying to get some courage from somewhere to get this monkey off my back.

'I will propose to her when I reach that big oak tree,' I said to myself. I revised my target upon reaching the oak tree, 'I will tell when I reach that electric pole'. I was damn nervous on reaching the electric pole and thought, 'I will finally tell her when I reach the tea stall' which was some 20 meters ahead of us.' Nothing really happened; I just kept pushing the target from one object to another and couldn't say any of the words I had carefully selected. Sheena was a smart girl and she had sensed this huge amount of anxiety in me.

"Hope all is well."

"Yeah, perfectly fine."

"You seem too pre-occupied, as if you are solving some complex physics numerical from one of those Russian books ..... or something even more complicated."

"Nah, there is nothing in my mind."

"Ok, then drop me home."

It was the most frustrating drive of my life as far as I can remember; I wanted to say so much but ended up saying nothing. It was not just a matter of today; I was not able express myself for so many days. We reached her house, which was a huge colonial army bungalow of a celebrated Major General, flushed with extra security and duly guarded by the sepoys of the Indian Army.

As usual, I dropped her at the main gate of the bungalow, where these four guards would always look at me with suspicion and a bit of un-required, self generated protective half-brotherly feeling towards Sheena.

She got down from my bike and looked at me with a cute but very angry expression and said, "I have not seen an idiot like you."

"Why?"

"You will spend all your life evaluating what to say? When to say? And how to say?"

"What are you saying?"

"You very well know what I am saying; you are a king of melodrama but a big zero in real expression."

"Hey Sheena, but I am sure you have felt it, it is just a different matter that I have not been able to put it in words."

"Bunk it, you are a nut."

Feeling confident suddenly, I held her hands in front of a very small fraction of the Indian Army and said,

"I love you sweetheart and am totally addicted to you. You give me a kick which takes my life to a different high. I either need you now or need rehabilitation for curing my addiction. Tell me what do I get?"

Sheena hurriedly snatched her hand away from mine, "We

must have gone on a date some 77,000 times and you have selected the perfect setting for expressing your love – outside my house in front of 4 soldiers. Now please go, it would have been a better idea if I had proposed to you. At least I would have made it more romantic."

"I am sorry baby, but you know I love you."

"Bye, now go away, call me in the night."

Well, this was how horrendously I actually proposed to my first girlfriend outside her house spurred on by her. Nevertheless, it was the beginning of a great relationship. And yes, I did call her that night and even recited a poem which I had written for her.

Things just got better from then on, the exams went well and our results were even better. There was more of Sheena in my life, more of love and of course our first kiss near the oak tree where I originally thought of proposing to her.

"It was an absolute cardamom kiss," I said

"Now what is that?"

"That's your flavor and your freshness, just like a green cardamom."

"Now again you have started."

"Yeah, it has just started. Now is the turn for another kiss; a peppermint flavour."

Followed by her nudge and a push. And then her usual request.

"Now please drop me home and call me at night. Bye and Good night."

Chapter 9 (D)

Love Pentagon

Four deserving young lads and one pretty girl is a deadly combination. You don't need to be a rank holder in chemistry to know what happens when sulfuric acid is poured on sodium. Sheetal was no less than sulfuric acid; or in direct words, she was very hot and very deadly. We were no less than Sodium, Potassium, Lithium and Francium just waiting to come in contact with her and cause the explosion.

Before I go fast forward, let me go back a little. The meeting point of the four metals and acid was not in a laboratory but at the New Delhi railway station. All four of us were going back to Pune for our final semester of MBA and Sheetal was travelling back to Pune as well to complete her last semester of Master's in mass communication. As a matter of chance, we happened to meet inside the train. While this sort of thing happens very often in Hindi movies where the hero meets the heroine, it occurs very rarely in real life. In my six years of student life, such a thing had never happened before.

Saurabh, Jitu, Puneet and I were best of friends. Puneet was obscenely philosophical for his age, Saurabh was handsome and a thorough gentleman, Jitu was a stud with lots of energy and I can probably (at maximum) be classified as cute and funny. We all had our areas of strength and enough reasons for hoping for the best. Coming back to the train journey, as a matter of practice, the reservation list is put up outside the railway compartment in India. Going by the age old human conditioning, every Indian tends to check his / her before boarding the train. Most of the time, we were surrounded by men. Once I remember there was a female passenger, but she was 71. Grandmamma turned out to be more of a liability during the journey.

This time it was different, the name read read Sheetal Khanna F 22 on the list. This girl was extremely pretty, smart and confident. She had the average height of an Indian girl, but had striking features with a clear fair complexion, long thick brown hair and nice black eyes which had sparkle and shine. In fact, this time it was even more different, Puneet happened to know her, although very casually. His father and her father were colleagues in the Indian Army and they had briefly met a couple of times in the officers club.

"Hi Sheetal, what are you doing here?" Puneet always had this knack of asking silly questions.

"I have come here to see you off," she said.

"Ha ha, are you also going to Pune?"

"No I am going to Mount Everest. Of course Puneet, you know that I am doing my course from Pune, we discussed it when we met in the club the other day."

"Oh yeah, I can get into unnecessary questions. Even professional answering machines like professors can sometimes get fed up with my questions."

"You should be happy he didn't ask you your name again," Jitu butted in.

Puneet introduced all four of us and this was probably the first major social benefit work he had ever done in his life.

"So how were the holidays?" quizzed Puneet

"Great as ever, didn't see you much in the club."

"I had joined a yoga course and then later enrolled for a meditation camp. I like to spend time on different kind of activities."

"That's unbelievable for guys of your age to do all this sort of things. I had a blast, no discipline like you guys, just fun."

"Please don't generalize, I find it very embarrassing. Puneet is the only philosopher in our group," I had to pitch in, I felt as if I had the sole responsibility to save the persona of an average twenty-two-year-old guy.

"That's great, holidays had better be fun."

"Life should better be fun, holidays or in college," I said.

"Totally agree."

"Sheetal, are you from Delhi?" I asked.

"Yeah, currently from Delhi. Dad is posted there, how about you?"

"I am from Dehradun."

"Dehradun! What a coincidence, Dad was posted there for 5 years in Indian Military Academy (IMA), we just moved to Delhi about 6 months back."

"No wonder, this pretty face looked very familiar."

"Are you serious?" she asked.

"Just kidding."

But jokes apart, whenever two persons from Dehradun

meet outside, there is an immediate connect. Those who have lived in this beautiful valley will surely understand my sentiments.

"I was there for the passing out parade in IMA this year, it is always a great sight," I said

"It is truly symphony at its best. There is something regal about the whole ceremony."

"I like army men," she continued.

"Then you will surely like Jitu, we call him colonel."

"Ah Colonel, why so?"

"Because they think I exercise too much, I love adventure sports, like mountain climbing and of course I like a little bit of Old Monk on weekends," Jitu said.

"Colonel sounds nice."

"Yeah, even better if you can be one without having to join army."

"But real colonels are real."

"But they can never be 22," said Jitu.

"You have a good sense of humor too," she added.

"You are the quietest one," she pointed towards Saurabh.

"Not really, that can just be an early impression."

"Will you have coffee?" Saurabh asked her.

"I don't mind," she said.

"I have two hands; I am getting one coffee for her and one for myself. Anyone else who wants coffee will have to come along with me to the pantry."

"I will come with you," said Puneet, acting as a true philanthropist.

"A little extra strong for me," I made my preference clear.

"For me too, those who like old monk can't have light coffee," added Jitu.

"Strong one for me too, those who like army men like strong coffee too." Sheetal chipped in as well.

"Great. Strong coffee is a common thread amongst all of us," said Saurabh

"Strong coffee is not good in the long run; it has a lot of caffeine. Light food and light drinks is a key to good health." This of course had to be Puneet.

"You sound so much like my father. You must meet him in the club over a healthy bowl of chicken clear soup," suggested Sheetal.

Puneet stayed quiet, but was visibly irritated. Being compared to her father was not a good beginning, unless her father was Pierce Brosnan, which he was not. It was a very common problem with Puneet, his first seven days interaction with any girl were always related to yoga, health, meditation and philosophy in general.

"Clear vegetable soup would be fine, as I don't eat chicken. I can also tell you the advantages of green vegetables and spiritual reasons for not having chicken," Puneet replied after recovering from the father effect.

"Not today please."

It is good to be spiritual, but is a sin to be consistently boring. It is the law of interaction particularly suitable at a certain age. Puneet was yet to learn this. But I guess, he might have good female following when he is fifty, unless he chooses to renounce the world by then.

"By the way, I can't get three cups of coffee as well," Puneet realised after a while.

"Jitu, why don't you go with them," I said.

"Just don't feel like moving."

"Ok Colonel, you can rest, I will play the Good Samaritan today."

Jitu looked at me with a smile and loads of naughtiness in his eyes, which clearly suggested he didn't want us to come back soon.

"Well, my grandfather was in the army too," Jitu said immediately after we left, trying to build on the Army connection.

"That's great, but that must be long back."

"Oh yeah, India wasn't even independent at that time. I have heard stories of World War II from my grandfather. He fought in the war and was a hero, at least that's what he always claimed."

"There are never any heroes in a war. There are only losers. I agree with what Plato said 'only the dead have seen the end of the war'. The misery of war continues with the families of the dead. Wars are so regressive. It is a man's obsession over man made boundaries."

Jitu did not utter a word; he had been trying to impress her.

"The quest for power is insatiable, even the great Alexander left empty handed. He just didn't leave empty handed, but he also left dead, beaten and bruised soldiers and their unfortunate families," she continued.

Jitu was confused, for him the army meant war and war meant valour.

"I agree. I meant I liked the passion of people in the army, not exactly fond of wars myself."

"Then why didn't you join the army?" she asked.

"I want to be an investment banker. I am here to live and not exist. Money holds the key. I have some dreams and the chosen route is right."

"'Money is a by product; you should just do what you like. Don't chase a hazy vision because it looks greener from a distance. Anyway, we all have our perspective. But money is not everything in life," she said.

"I have heard that too, money is not everything, after all there is Visa and MasterCard. Just joking, but for me the destination matters and not the route," he replied.

"For me the journey is the key. You may take twenty years to reach your destination, but then you can't get your twenty years back. I want to be in a creative field because I enjoy the creative process and that's why I am doing all this. Money and fame is not on my mind. If it is meant to be a reward of my work, it will come. My dreams come from my heart and my heart is in the right place," she defended her view point.

"My heart is on the left side where it is meant to be. I guess I also operate too much out of the left hemisphere of my brain. For me logic and reasoning is supreme, everything else is good enough for a Sunday brunch discussion," said Jitu with a bit of impatience.

"Cool. I must meet you more on Sundays in that case," she said putting an end to the discussion.

Jitu was not hitting the right chords; it often happens with hulks like him.

"Here's your coffee Miss Sheetal Khanna."

"Thanks."

"So what are you studying in Pune?" asked Saurabh.

"Final semester of mass communication."

"Wow. The pursuit of something creative; sounds interesting."

"Let us see how it shapes up," she replied.

"Focusing more on films or advertising?"

"Well, either one really, advertising looks like an easier entry. I did my summer project with a leading agency. In fact I am doing another project for them in Pune. I am hoping to start from copy writing and then move ahead from there as I go along."

"All the best, when you are clear with your desires, they all just come true. I feel like a creative person myself, but I have chosen the much treaded path of doing my master's in finance. Ideally I would love to be a film maker," added Saurabh.

"Then what is stopping you?"

"Nothing really, I guess my conditioning. My dad is a CEO of a leading multinational company and my mother is a school principal. I have been academically conditioned since my teenage days to be taking a dive into the corporate world. My own realization for creative pursuits is a recent one and I am sure I will follow it in my own way. It is practical that I do what I have been chasing since many years and create an alternative way for myself as I go along," replied Saurabh.

"I like your approach, there is a bit of practicality and bit of wild search," she reiterated.

"It is time to search for my book and get on with that," said Saurabh.

Saurabh had a huge penchant for reading and occupied the upper berth with his John Grisham thriller. He could spend

16 hours out of a 20 hour journey by sleeping and reading his books on the upper berth.

"Sometimes I wonder whether John Grisham is his real friend," it had to be Jitu and his remark found no response.

"How is uncle doing?" Sheetal asked Puneet.

"He is fine. He might get posted out of Delhi."

"Ok. Where is he likely to be posted?'

"It is expected to be Mhow. I like small cities, Delhi and its madness gets onto my nerves," he said.

"I guess so, I miss Dehradun too. But I like Delhi as well; it is a juicy place in a different sort of way."

"It has great shopping, great food, and lots of greenery. On the flip side, it has too much display of materialism, power and politics," she went on.

"Politics reminds me of upcoming elections. Which party do you think will come to power?" Puneet got back to strange topics that he discusses in the first week as described earlier.

"I am not interested in politics."

"As good citizens, we must follow general elections at least."

"Hmmm."

"I think there will be a hung parliament this time."

"It seriously doesn't affect me."

"But a hung parliament is not good for our economy at this stage and it will affect you in some way," Puneet got hung on the idea of a hung parliament.

"Puneet, move over it. Fruits keep hanging from trees; clothes keep hanging on the hangers and boys keep hanging outside the girl's hostel. There are enough hanging items in the universe. We can add one more hung parliament to the entire gamut of already hanging objects. It should not be that big a problem." I had no choice but to divert the topic a little before Puneet could have plunged into discussing the biographies of the electoral candidates.

"It seems like a practical suggestion," agreed Sheetal.

"I hate train journeys," Jitu remarked.

"Especially the long ones get particularly irritating," she said.

"This is the last semester of studying; I guess once we start working, a lot of these issues will get automatically tackled. I am particularly judicious about spending my father's money; hopefully I will travel more often by air once I start earning myself," he added.

"Where do you stay in Pune?" I asked her.

"In the girl's hostel of the university."

"We are neighbours in that case; our college is right next to the university. This is too much of a coincidence; the Dehradun connection, same train, same city and now your hostel is right next to mine," I said.

"Yeah. The world is a small place," she commented.

"By the way George Gilbert must be in your batch," she quickly added.

"Oh yes, I know he is from Dehradun too."

"He is a very good friend of mine and an extremely creative person," I said.

"Of course he is. We are doing the winter project together. We are making a small film on campus life," she said.

"He was mentioning it to me. In fact, George has promised me a small role in it. Now that you guys are working together, I don't mind giving an audition right now."

"It would be the first ever audition in a train," she said.

"May be the first audition, but Indian trains always have enough display of talent with so many beggars singing film songs all the time."

"I really pity those poor boys, they are so underprivileged," she replied.

"Life is unfair for sure. Anyway, let's not divert too much and am looking forward to confirmation of my role," I insisted on sealing my role.

"Sure. We need actors and I can't say no if George has agreed. What are your plans after passing out, just heard from Jitu that he wants to be an investment banker."

"I am specializing in marketing, hoping for a break in financial services or software marketing. I would prefer to be in new economy business. Let us see how opportunities shape up," I said.

"And what about you Puneet? Please don't tell me that you want to join an NGO," she asked.

"I would love to work for an NGO, but satisfaction is not everything in life. We live in a utilitarian world and I need to be more commercial in my approach, at least in my career," replied Puneet.

"Thank God, I was dreading that you would say that you want to join a nonprofit organization and then dedicate the rest of your life to rural India."

"Not now. But I would certainly contribute some day in some way for sure," he said in a very clear voice.

Sheetal was an interesting girl, very witty, very sharp in counter attacking you and, of course, an easy going fun loving girl with a creative bent of mind.

The rounds of discussions continued as the journey continued. While it took another twenty hours to reach the destination, I would like to sum up a few points to describe the events that took place in the remaining journey.

- All four of us took her telephone number in such a way that neither of us were aware that the remaining three had also taken it from her.
- She might have realized that all four of us had taken her number separately at an opportune time during the journey but she also did not let this thing be known out at large.
- Jokes apart and keeping aside the budding aspirations across the board, we were a bunch of nice guys and I am sure she too enjoyed our company and we took good care of her as best you can do to near strangers that would soon turn into friends.

College began as soon as the journey ended. The summary of the first three days of college after the journey is mentioned below for quick absorption:

- We did not bunk a single lecture, however boring they might have been.
- There was hardly a change in anything after the holidays, which is usually the case with colleges and professors. Professor Pinto continued his monotone teachings in exactly the same nasal voice, speaking at the same wavelength for two consecutively hours. If you were to plot his sound waves, you would find that there were no crests and troughs, but only a single straight line at the same frequency. If I have to make an analogy, his voice

was like that faulty public address system which by error sends out that shrieky, screechy sound signal creating a sharp, piercing and an alarming noise which irritates you no end. But yes, the important thing is that we still attended all those lectures.

- The food in the mess was as inedible as ever.
- In all the three days, the four of us never discussed Sheetal at all.
- The only difference was that we were looking forward to the weekend and probably thinking of fixing up a date or rather a semi date (to put it in right perspective) with her.

I was the first one to call her up on Wednesday evening.

"Hello Sheetal, Jas Anand here."

"Hey Jas, what's up? How have you guys been?"

"We are doing well. College is as mechanical as ever and hostel is great fun like always. What about you?"

"We have just started our work on the film and we are in the process of finalizing our script. And yes, your role is small but interesting."

"Great. What's your plan for Saturday? If there is nothing much planned, let's meet in the evening for coffee?"

"Nothing much as yet, it should be okay; let us meet at 6 p.m. at the Deccan Coffee House."

"Fantastic. I will be there six minutes before six."

"Sharp six will also be good enough."

"Six minutes to six sounds nice to say," I gave my marketing oriented logic.

"Hey, before you hang up, would any of your friends be interested in coming as well?"

"They could be, but I guess let's, keep the plan this way. We can always meet up in a group later," I blocked the possibility of a public rally.

"Okay." she agreed.

We hung up; I was glad that the meeting was fixed and there was a 6 centimetre bounce in my walk for about 6 seconds.

You might call it a coincidence or predictive behavioral pattern of men, that Puneet was the next to call her on the same day after one hour.

"Hi Sheetal, How are you?"

"Hi Puneet, I am doing good."

"I was actually wondering that it has been long time since we have met," he said.

"Honestly, we just met on Sunday and it has just been three days, not really a long time unless you insist."

"On second thoughts, the 'long time' logic is quite flawed," he seemed to embarrassingly agree with her.

"That's ok, but what exactly were you wondering?" she was in a mood for some fun.

"Not wondering anything in particular, rather I was wandering in my thought process."

"Wonderful or should I say wanderful."

"Actually, I was wondering if you would be free this Saturday, there is a very interesting handicrafts exhibition in Pune exhibiting the handicrafts made by tribes of Tripura."

"Handicrafts exhibition, that doesn't sound like my Saturday plan."

"There is also an Indian classical dance festival where we can go, where the kids from an orphanage from the interiors Assam will be performing live."

"While Indian classical dance is a great art form and it being performed by under privileged children is indeed laudable, but again it is something that doesn't excite me to go all the way to see it," she turned this one down too.

"There is also a new museum which is getting inaugurated on Saturday. A brand new museum with age old objects sounds like a perfect blend of old and new. Does it sound okay to you?" begged Puneet nearly praying for an approval.

"Puneet, let us meet up sometimes for a cup of coffee and we can always plan something that interests both of us at a later date."

"Ok, how about Saturday evening for a cup of coffee?"

"Saturday evening is a little tied up."

"Saturday dinner?" was his counter offer.

"We will surely catch up for dinner; we can jointly fix with your other friends and meet at a convenient date."

"That's a good idea, but I was keen to meet you without them; but of course your dinner suggestion is indeed very nice," he said.

"Okay, let us talk tomorrow and see how we can fix it."

She must be amused by now that both of us wanted to meet her without friends. Anyway, she had fixed the time with me and had kept Puneet on hold for now.

You may again call it a coincidence or the same old behavioral pattern theory that Jitu was the third person to call her on the same night.

"Comrade Sheetal, colonel Jitu reporting."

"Tango to Charlie. How are you doing Jitu?"

"I am doing well. But I have been feeling terrible about having offered you terrible coffee in the train," Jitu took off.

"Then you must very quickly make amends, so do you want to meet for a coffee on this Saturday?" she asked him very quickly.

"Exactly. I called you precisely for that; it is amazing how you asked me before I could."

"Ok, you would like to meet alone or come with your friends."

"We have terrifically same wavelength; let us meet alone and we can meet in a group some other time," he replied.

"Fantastic, are you free at six?"

"I am free from 4.30 p.m onwards, at your service always."

"Six is fine, let us meet at Deccan Coffee House."

"I can pick you from your hostel," he offered.

"No. I will meet you there at six."

She was finding this funny and was planning a funny plot to expose all of us. It was also a great test of internal communications between four good friends. Jitu was also mighty surprised, that the plan was fixed before he uttered a word. He would probably credit it to a strong telepathic connection between him and Sheetal till he discovered…

She called up Puneet, "My plans have changed; we can meet at six on Saturday for coffee. Are you free?"

"Of course, where should we meet?"

"It is always Deccan Coffee House."

"I think they make the best coffee in town and their Ethiopian beans are good for health too. I will be there at six sharp," he said.

The predictable behavioral patterns theory has a lot of merit; it may get delayed in some cases but chances are bright that the expected behavior deviation will not be more than 48 hours. Saurabh did not need 48 hours; in fact he called her on Thursday morning, exactly 12 hours after my call.

"Hi, what's up?"

"The sky."

"This is a very silly, a very old and stupid reply. I didn't expect this from you," he snapped back at her.

"Then what did you expect?"

"Better than this. You are a creative person, you can be better than this."

"I will be more original next time."

"Let me come to the point, you owe me several coffees that I bought for you in the train. Just kidding; I will be really glad if you can meet for a cup of coffee in a coffee shop where I can sit with you peacefully and not worry about the train bumps."

"Okay."

"How about Saturday?" he checked with her.

"Saturday is fine."

"What time?" he asked her.

"Now that depends."

"Depends on what?" he was a little confused.

"You will not understand that. You just tell me whether you want to meet me alone or your friends will also come along?" she asked him.

"We usually go out together, but I guess not this time. But yes, we must surely meet together some other time."

"In that case, the time is 6 p.m and the venue is Deccan Coffee House," she said.

"And in that case, I want to thank you for giving your time and in that case I am also thankful to you for choosing the coffee shop as well," Saurabh butted in.

In that case, none of us knew what she knew. Time is known to fly faster than a jet and before we knew, it was Saturday. All four of us were very particular in planning our Saturdays in advance, but this time was different. There was no mention of making any plan at all by any of us.

We came back to the hostel from the college on Saturday afternoon and the scene that unfolded was something like this:

- There was no conversation between us; a common thread of silence connected us.
- All four of us shaved at the same time and applied the after shave lotion generously.
- All four of us removed our best colognes and sprayed them liberally right from the neck line to our hands and even to the shirts and handkerchiefs for back up.
- We changed our shirts a few times before selecting the final one and sprayed the cologne once again on the winning selection.
- There was still no discussion while all this drama was taking place.

"Puneet, what is your plan for the evening?" I asked him reluctantly.

"Nothing really."

"Then why are you getting ready like this? You have nearly emptied half your cologne bottle."

"Actually I was thinking of going to the handicrafts exhibition."

"Who are you going with?"

"I would prefer to go alone; spend time at ease seeing the handicrafts. We come alone in this world and go back alone, so what is the harm in going to the exhibition all alone?"

"Ok, as you please. It is important to spend time with oneself once in a while," I said.

"Yeah, I agree, meditative weekend as I call it. Not just that, my love for handicrafts is immense and I am excited to go there. What is your plan?"

"My cousin is coming to Pune; I will meet him in the evening and will be back after spending some time with him."

"Ok, great. See you at night."

"Jitu, what is your plan for the evening?" I checked with him.

"One of my relatives is not keeping well; I have to see him in the Ruby Hall Hospital."

"I did not know that you even had a relative in Pune; never saw you visiting him earlier."

"Actually, he is a distant relative. I may not have visited him in good times, but I think we must show support and solidarity in bad times. Besides, my mother is very keen that I should meet him."

"Solidarity and support is the best reflection of the care you can show as a relative. How old is he and what is the problem?" asked Puneet.

"He is around 67 and he has developed very chronic lacuna distontics of the small intestine with a simultaneous dichotomic neurologus of the large intestines combined with severe inflammation of throat duct with a biodegradation of the kidney skin. I think the matter is serious."

"Sounds serious for sure. Can you repeat the disease again?" I asked.

"The name of disease is not important, what really matters is the deadliness of the complicated disease. I am very tense and not in a mood to repeat the name," Jitu cleared his stand.

"Then you must go, but why are you wearing such flashy clothes with an overdose of cologne; it is totally out of place for a hospital and even more when it involves a terribly deadly sounding disease. Go and immediately get a sober dress," I reprimanded him.

"I have heard my uncle is a positive person and he hates dullness. My dressing is a tribute to his vibrant life and a good smell is important for beating the dirty hospital odor," he defended his attire and accessories vehemently.

"By the way, which cousin of yours is coming?" Jitu asked me diverting the topic.

"He is a distant cousin; in fact, he also lives at a distant place. He runs a dispensary for the poor people in Mogadishu, the capital city of Somalia and keeps travelling to arrange the funds to run the medical care centre for the needy. Ranjeet has dedicated his entire life to humanity and he has come along with a delegation of a development agency for fund raising initiative in Mumbai and Pune. I consider it my privilege to meet such a cousin," I had to say something.

I could sense an orgasmic expression on Puneet's face; for him this would be an ideal life and meeting such a person could be a life changing dimension.

"I would love to meet him, can you fix a lunch with him tomorrow?" he requested me

My cousin was as fictitious as Alice in wonderland; I had to find an excuse because Puneet has a solid knack to get sticky on such matters.

"Puneet, he will keep coming to India for fund raising. I will make you meet him the next time for sure," I said.

"I can't wait to meet such an exceptional man of dedication and humanitarian spirit; I just can't wait till the next visit," he said.

"Why don't you cancel your visit to the handicrafts exhibition and join Jas today evening itself," remarked Saurabh in his ever fact of matter manner.

"But my mind is totally geared up for a handicrafts exhibition."

"You exhibition can be seen tomorrow, it is there for one more week," said Saurabh.

"Jas, I can meet your cousin today for dinner or for a coffee after that," said Puneet.

"But my cousin does not meet strangers at dinner time. There is too much violence in Africa and hence he is scared of new people in the night. It will be very unfair on my part to propose this knowing his fears and apprehensions," I had to say something.

"But I am not a stranger, I am your friend," he said.

"For him, everyone is a stranger. In fact, he has even asked me to carry my own identity card and a printout of his email as a backup proof." I had to say something to save the situation.

"Your cousin is very strange," said an obviously puzzled and irritated Saurabh.

"Of course. He left the plush job in a top hospital in Singapore to move to Somalia. Such people are very rare and are sometimes very strange," I had to say something to save the situation.

"Then can I meet him for lunch tomorrow?" said Puneet, he was adamant.

"Unfortunately, he is leaving early in the morning for Mumbai. He loves to travel early morning. He has this habit of leaving before sunrise and he always welcomes a new day in the new city. Saurabh is right, he is indeed very strange." I had to say something to save the situation, yet again.

"How do you know so much about him?" asked a curious Saurabh.

"I write a lot of emails to him and he keeps telling me about his life and its philosophies." I had to say something to save the situation, for god's sake and mine.

"It is a moment of great confusion for me. Should I meet a great Indian doctor from Somalia or appreciate the work of Indians in Tripura. I think Tripura is more relevant at this moment," said Puneet.

"All three of you are behaving in a really weird fashion. One is going to meet a weird cousin with weird habits. The other one is going for a weird handicrafts exhibition and the third one is going to meet a relative who had no trace till yesterday and today he has suddenly emerged from nowhere having developed a weird sounding disease. I really find it stupid and honestly a bit fishy too," Saurabh summarized his observation.

"What is your plan?" I asked Saurabh.

"Honestly, my plan is very simple. I am meeting a friend of mine for coffee," he replied.

"Which friend?" I interrogated.

"I will tell you guys when I come back; that is all I can say," said Saurabh, who was by far the most truthful about the whole episode. Except for taking the name of the girl, he was speaking the truth.

"Great. Have fun." I said.

All four of us left nearly at the same time on our respective bikes. All rivers lead to the sea and so were we all heading towards Sheetal. The impact of mild lies and importance of mild truths can be seen at best in such circumstances. A little bit of truth or a little less of lies could have made our evening far more respectful. Even if you don't know Newton's law of motion or have no clue about the concept of speed and velocity, it is still easy to believe that usually when people leave at the same time, they tend to reach the destinations at the same time, provided they are headed for the same place.

As I was walking towards the Deccan Coffee House, I saw someone who resembled Puneet and with a little more concentration, I realized that this man in fact looked like Puneet and was even wearing the same clothes. Before I could analyze it further, this man saw me too and immediately turned around 180 degrees on his toes. I have seen many cars take an absurd U-turn, but this was the first time I saw a walking man take such a rash and an ugly U-turn.

I was really surprised and confused at the same time. I was looking left and right in a state of confusion. On the left glance, I saw a man who resembled Jitu and on the right I saw someone who looked like Saurabh. Before I could look or confirm anything further, both these men took a wild cut and disappeared into some shops. Once again, at the cost of repetition, I must say that I have seen many cars taking rash and careless cuts on the roads, but it was the first time I saw average walking men do the same.

"Driving licenses are a passé, I think we need licenses to walk on the road," I thought to myself.

The next five minutes were filled with lots of quick twists and turns, with a strong resemblance to the hide and seek games which the kids play in childhood.

"Stop it, guys. Enough of pretending, turning and twisting," screamed Saurabh in the middle of the road.

"Who is pretending?" asked a concerned and curious passerby, a stranger.

"The three bastards you don't know," he replied in anger.

The stranger seeing his anger very quickly adopted a 'none of my business policy' and moved ahead.

I don't know when the Golden Quadrilateral project will be ready in India, but this Golden Quadrilateral of four best friends entered the Deccan Coffee House feeling stupid and ridiculous.

Sheetal was waiting at the table near the entrance with a digital camera in her hand.

"It is a rare moment; it has to be captured," she said laughing uncontrollably.

It was an expose like the ones many news channel keep showing. We were angry, embarrassed and feeling really stupid. Saurabh was red with anger, I was blue with shame, Jitu was pink with embarrassment and Puneet was yellow on facing the reality. The furniture was brown and the backdrop paint was light green. This was truly a one of the most colorful photographs ever taken on earth.

"Is this a coincidence or a communication failure or is it

connivance on our part?" asked a visibly shaken Puneet.

"Let us order coffee and quickly get out of here," Saurabh meant business.

"I have read *My Experiments with Truth* by Mahatma Gandhi and even he has admitted to his lies. I admit that I have lied about the pretext of handicrafts exhibition," continued Puneet trying to dissect the situation further.

"Thanks Puneet for admitting, otherwise I would have been hallucinating that you are still in the exhibition admiring the handicrafts made some talented tribals of Tripura," I chipped in with a bit of irritation.

"I think it was a communication failure of the highest order," remarked Jitu.

"I think it is really a cute and sweet episode. Trust me guys, I just did it for fun and you guys involuntarily made it easier for me to pull this one off. I like you guys; otherwise I wouldn't have become friendly with strangers. You know girls have a good sixth sense and I am sure you are nice guys. Now stop sulking and feeling stupid about this incident, just take it lightly and enjoy this moment with a nice coffee. Deccan Coffee House is the best; right Puneet?" She had sensed that some of us were totally pissed off.

"Yes. It has best quality coffee beans imported from Ethiopia with less caffeine as well. But, why did this communication failure take place?" said Puneet still mulling over the matter.

"Enough guys, let us analyze this in our hostel," said Saurabh with firmness in his voice.

"Relax Saurabh," said Sheetal.

"Honestly, it is your fault too. I will appreciate if we leave this topic aside." said Saurabh.

"Four coffees as quickly as you can," Jitu got wild at the waiter.

"Sir, would you like it with cream or prefer a particular flavour?" the waiter was programmed to ask some extra questions for generating some extra revenue.

"Get it plain, get it very fast and dare you ask half a question more," Jitu got wilder.

"And please get the bill when you get the coffee, we are in a hurry," I made my contribution to the situation.

"Sorry guys, be a sport. We can't roll it back; just laugh it off," she insisted.

While there was a fair bit of awkwardness amongst us, she was very comfortable and made us feel at ease with the passage of time. Some women have this amazing quality of being warm and soothing; they can make your moods swing back to normalcy with their grace and charm. Sheetal acted like a balm and needless to say, I like such women who can make a man feel cozy in their presence. It is a very non macho outlook perhaps, but something which I personally look forward to in a woman.

"Ok madam, we apologize for the confusion and for our not so gentlemanly behaviour," said Saurabh.

"Apologies aside, the tone and the texture sounds better now," she looked a little relaxed after seeing all of us behaving normally.

So then, we eased out during the cup of coffee, while Puneet stayed engulfed in truth, its interpretations and the communication failure / conspiracy theory. The only good part was that we parted on a positive note. Unanimously, we (including Sheetal) decided to eliminate this chapter from our history and agreed to believe that our first meeting in the train was the only meeting that ever took place.

Back to the hostel room; some unsettled energies had to be settled, the potential energy was ready to be converted into kinetic energy. It was the standard hostel room shared with 2 beds, 2 cupboards and 2 desks. The tube light was switched off and it was substituted by dimly lit study lamp creating the right ambience for further analysis.

4 guys, 4 cans of Kingfisher beer and 4 minds thinking on different lines.

Puneet started the conversation in a philosophical tone and body language, by lifting his left hand and bringing the can of beer near his left eye and very close to his forehead.

"What exactly went wrong?"

"You three bastards made a fool of us," remarked Saurabh.

"Nothing went wrong. Who would not want to spend time with a beautiful and a virtuous girl?" I said.

"It is the demand and supply problem; I wish we had met 4 girls in the train," Jitu contributed with his limited wisdom.

"The problem is not of supply, the problem is that of perfection we keep searching in a woman. Out of the four girls, I would still be pitching for Sheetal. If you find anyone better than her, then it is pure luck and a little bit of grace," I said.

"You are right, I can think of a better girl only in a fairly tale. She is nearly the best I have come across so far," Jitu chipped back.

"Best or the worst, why did you guys have to lie? Didn't I speak the part truth? We have been best of friends, why did we let this silly thing slip out of our control?" Saurabh was still disturbed about the incident.

"Forget it Saurabh, think of the positive side; a 67 year old man is no longer dying in Ruby Hall Clinic," I said.

"Think of the negative side, there is one doctor less working for the poor people is Somalia," replied Saurabh.

"By the way, what was that fucking disease that you invented for the old man?" I wanted to double check with Jitu.

"That nomenclature technique is called as random combination of superlatives along with some parts of body. When spoken at length for a long time, the output that you get is a complicated disease," Jitu clarified.

"Why Somalia and why not Sierra Leone? How do you guys make a choice in such matters?" asked Saurabh, who had real allergies to even mild lies.

"It is called as 'top of the mind' recall in terms of marketing concept. Besides that, Mogadishu and Somalia sounds more like an authentic choice. But jokes apart, someday I will really ensure that I make an effort to do some good work in Somalia. Now that this thought has come to me I should contribute in this lifetime." I reflected on my good side and made a promise for the future.

We had some serious fun about the entire episode including the twists and turns we all took near the Deccan Coffee House. While we were having a blast poking fun at each other, Puneet was still lost in some thoughts.

"This is not a joke, this is a potential problem," said Puneet.

"Now what?" demanded Jitu.

"Can't you see all four of us are interested in her? Is that not a potential problem?" asked Puneet.

"No, it is not," replied Saurabh.

"I agree with Saurabh. It is just the beginning of a friendship; I think it is stupid to think on those lines. Besides you can never create architecture from a relationship. Relationship is something which gets formed automatically," I added my bit.

"Besides, how do you know what she wants? She might even have a boyfriend," Jitu also pounced on Puneet.

"She is a nice girl; let's leave it at that," remarked Saurabh.

"Once a very lovely friend of mine had advised me to cherish everything that you have in the present and not worry about the future. Let's cherish our lives the way they are, if she or anyone else is destined to make an entry, we will start cherishing that as well," I concluded.

"Good night guys."

The semester rolled over very well. The remaining bit can be summarized in the following manner:

- There was strong focus on studies and securing good placements. And it happened.
- There were lots of group dinners and coffees with Sheetal.
- There were lots of individuals meetings with her; often need based and situation based.
- Yes, there was a lot of transparency amongst all of us.
- Lastly, I was by far in maximum contact with her as I had done a small role in the film titled "College Cacophony".
- I was certain that she did not have a boyfriend.

At the end of the semester, all five of us were in bag packing mode to move on to the next phase of life. Three of us were heading to Mumbai and two were heading back to Delhi. And amidst planning all the futuristic projections, I got a call from Sheetal.

"I want to meet you for a coffee. Alone and this evening itself. Something really important to tell you and you better come alone," she said.

"What is that you want to tell me?" I enquired.

"I can't say it on the phone; let's meet and talk. Some sort of a confession," she hung up

Guys, I am not Larry Love. But I am not an inert gas either. It was like a sudden clash of thunder and I could not think of anything else. I was sure that she wanted to confess something important and my mind was fairly predictive about a brewing relationship ahead.

I discussed it with Jitu; he was sure that she liked me and it had to be a confession of love / proposal of love / acknowledgment of special feelings or any other derivatives derived on these lines.

I had done a winter project with a reputed company and had just received Rs. 8000 as remuneration for it. It was a big amount in those days. Jitu insisted that I should buy a nice gift for her.

"All four tried; you are the lucky bastard. Let us go and buy a gift for her from your stipend," said Jitu.

Both of us rushed off to Main Street and bought a really cool Tissot wrist watch for her pouring out my last penny.

It was a mild winter evening and I had dressed as best as I could. I had this awesome black leather jacket which I wore on my denim jeans. Apart from being black and original leather, it had a big pocket inside in which the wrist watch could hide comfortably.

The whole "scene to be" was rehearsed and Jitu had personally choreographed each move for me. I was supposed to synchronize my hand movement with her confession of love. As per the script, the moment she would admit her love I would remove the gift and tell her, "I love you too".

Everything was in place. The watch, woman and the man.

She came like a breeze; like a westerly wind.

"I cannot wait; I really have to tell you something very important," she said I was standing confidently and in my heart of hearts I could feel a resonance saying "Come on baby, now say it."

"You know Jas, I love Saurabh. But the problem is that he is so reserved unlike you and Jitu, so I am not sure whether feelings are mutual? You are such a close friend so I thought I would consult you on this. Semester is over and time is running out," she was quick to spill the beans. It came as a huge blow; time was indeed running out and like it happens in cricket, I was literally "run out". I felt tremors as if a big meteor had just hit the earth and the immediate next thought was that I have already spent eight thousand rupees on the watch. And the worst part was that I really did not know whether the shop had a replacement policy.

Well, the situation demanded an immediate transition from a jolted lover to a loyal friend.

"I am sure he does," I replied with some poise and confidence.

"How do you know?" she said.

"My gut feeling at this moment tells me that; besides that I also know that I have never seen him take so much interest in any other girl in the last two years. Now don't waste time and let us go immediately to the hostel. I know him enough to know this," I replied.

Both of us sat on my bike and headed straight towards our hostel.

"With due respects, the lady can wait outside. There will be a stampede if you step into the boys' den. I will go inside and fetch your man," I told her to wait outside the hostel.

"Bastard, you have been the chosen one. Sheetal is in love with you," I told Saurabh.

"Why? Has BBC broadcasted it?" he was not amused.

"The BBC is Sheetal herself. She just mentioned it to me. She was unsure about your feelings so she mildly consulted me on this," I replied.

Saurabh smiled. He looked happy; his matured persona kept his happiness in check though. And he rushed out to meet her.

"Wait!" I said.

"Now what happened?" Saurabh asked me.

"Please take this Tissot watch and go. This is for Sheetal," I told him.

"But from where did this watch come?" he enquired with a fairly puzzled expression.

"It is a long story; I will explain it later," I replied.

"Oh, I understood," Saurabh summed up the situation in his mind.

Saurabh took the watch reluctantly and went out.

Choreographer Jitu was quite shocked by the anticlimax that happened.

"I have come to one conclusion," said Jitu in a pensive mood.

"Now what is the conclusion?" although I was really not interested.

"Girls prefer intense and mature guys. You and I are too funny to be taken seriously," he replied.

"You keep your conclusions with you. All I have learnt is that never buy expensive gifts till your girl demands or drives you up the wall," I chipped in with my pearl of accidental wisdom.

Saurabh came back after some time and in his mind he had figured out the 'Tissot watch sequence'.

"Sorry man, I did not know about your feelings," Saurabh said.

"All feelings have evaporated. All I remember is the money I paid for the watch. Let us make a deal," I said.

"What deal?" enquired Saurabh.

"If you end up marrying Sheetal then I will walk into your marriage without a gift," I said.

"Fair deal," replied Saurabh.

They indeed got married, and yes, I walked in empty handed to their marriage for I knew.

"You cannot gift a Tissot twice."

Section 3

Mind, intelligentsia and pseudo appeal

Fabio Fibmaster

If exaggeration is an art, then he is a genius like Leonardo Da Vinci; if exaggeration is a science, then he can be compared with Albert Einstein; and if cooking up stories is worth the palate, then he could well be the world's greatest chef ever.

When he got on with his fibbing, he had a unique talent of taking his cock and bull story to Himalayan heights. He was neither an evil guy nor an intentional fraud; he just had a disorder of cooking up stories for the sake of some trivial high. He was one of my room partners for a brief period during my bachelor days and I used to call him my 'laughter therapy' as everyday you could hear some utterly stupid and ridiculously unreliable fables. This laughter therapy was a great way to relieve stress at the end of the day.

He could accidently meet a girl at the bus stop while going to office and instead of reaching office he would actually reach her bedroom and make love to her. Fabio had a unique charisma of having 'sex with strangers' within the first few hours of meeting. The girls would drool to get a piece of him. With Fabio, possibilities got a new meaning.

Special features and tendencies:
- Master of trivial lies.
- Can possibly go to the moon for honeymoon through a secret NASA mission which no one will ever come to know of.
- Can keep fibbing exponentially, even more to defend his earlier lies.
- He was the brand ambassador of 'unintended humour'.

Another interesting aspect of Fabio was that he could be led into a trap of lying. All you had to do was to give him some start and a few lead indicators to weave a story. Fabio could come up with utter rubbish on the spot and for me, 'my laugher therapy' was on.

Let me elaborate the techniques of leading him into a trap. Just imagine a tired looking Fabio walking in very late in the night into the house. In reality and from the eyes of your conscience you can surely feel that he has had a tough day at work with a strong added possibility of having received some nasty comments from his boss. In a situation like this, all you have to do is to throw the bait and wait for him to catch it.

Me: Naughty boy, do you know what the time is?

Fabio: I know it is midnight.

Me: So, don't tell me that you are coming from office. Where have you been all this while?

(I know for sure that his boss has fired him twice and made him change the report at least three times. In reality, I could bet my life that he was coming from office.)

Fabio: Oh God, how do you guess it each time I go on a date?

Me: I can judge from your body language, so tell me who were you with?

Fabio: There was someone

Me: Who someone? Where did she suddenly emerge from?

Fabio: I had gone for a presentation to a client. Just got along famously with the IT manager there and we really got friendly in no time.

Me: And then?

Fabio: She just invited me for a beer to Leopold.

And this could go on. It was up to my decency totally to let this stop at beer or take this episode to a kiss or even extend it to the wildest sex two people could ever have. I have the highest respect for women and you can see that I have stopped at the beer cafe.

Yes, you could lead him into a trap and get yourself a good laugh. Fabio Fibmaster was truly the master of fibbing and trivial lies.

If you ever find him: Have fun!!! All you have to do is ask him some vague questions such as:

1. Do you know Barrack Obama by any chance?
2. Why don't you become an actor in Hollywood? You can be the best James Bond ever.
3. How many girlfriends do you have?

And you can expect terrific "Laughter Therapy".

Chapter 10 (B)

Can You Believe This?

Fabio had just returned from a business trip; he was visibly ultra excited and apparently bustling with lots of stories which were waiting to burst out.

Me: Hi Fabio, welcome back. How was your trip?

Fabio: Amazing, you will not believe what happened today.

Me (In my mind): Wow, time for laughter therapy.

Me (In real voice): I am a believer. Absolutely curious to know what happened.

Fabio: I got two surprises back to back on my return flight. First the airline upgraded me to business class (Airlines usually turn philanthropic when he is travelling). And you got to hear the second one carefully man; can you guess who sat next to me? The great Sachin Tendulkar, can you believe this?

Me: I told you I can believe anything.

Fabio: What a humble guy; so down to earth. It was a great flight for me.

Me: I am sure Sachin would have had a great time too.

(Please note I am leading him into a trap further, although he was the one to start this rubbish originally.)

Fabio: Of course, he was very happy to meet me too and discuss the intricacies of cricket. For one full hour we discussed how he could improve his batting further. Truly a master; he is so open to suggestions even after years of international cricket. It speaks volumes about his passion to learn.

Me: What suggestion did you give him?

Fabio: Lots of things such as balancing between aggression and defense. I also gave him some acting tips and voice modulation techniques for his advertisements.

Me: Amazing Fabio, you are simply brilliant. I am sure Sachin owes you a dinner for all the good advice you gave him.

Fabio: Very frankly, he indeed invited me over for dinner at his place.

Me: Very good, so when has he invited you? I will also come along. For the amount of good that you have caused him, I am sure he will entertain one extra guest as a matter of grace.

(It is only when you start converging to concrete points; that Fabio realizes the need to come off his tale.)

Fabio: The date was almost fixed; but then I have some business travel coming up so I could not confirm it during the flight. I will check with my boss and get back to him.

Me: Please call him tomorrow and fix the time. I am very keen to come.

And suddenly I saw Fabio frantically searching his pockets.

Fabio: Oh shit. Can you believe this?

Me: How many times do I have to tell you that I can believe anything?

Fabio: He had given me his mobile number on a piece of paper and I cannot find that paper. Is there a bigger fool than me? Can you believe this?

Just imagine the audacity, Sachin Tendulkar is inviting you for dinner at his house and our chap is waiting for a no objection certificate from his boss.

Just imagine the audacity once again, Sachin Tendulkar has given you his mobile number in his own handwriting on a piece of paper and you seem to lose it in the first hour itself.

But what to do; he is not Fabio Fibmaster without any reason. With Fabio, possibilities get a new meaning.

Yuvraj Singh does not know that he knows Fabio

It was the year 2000. Apart from the historic relevance it held from a Y2K perspective, for me it was a landmark year as Fabio was one of my room partners in this calendar year. It was an eye opening experience and before this I honestly did not know to what extent a human mind can go with its trivial lies.

I do not exactly remember the dates, but it must be in the middle of 2000 when the Indian cricket team was announced for the ICC knock out tournament in Kenya. Yuvraj Singh was one of the notable new selections for the tournament. While reading the newspaper, I came to know that Yuvraj Singh hailed from Chandigarh. Chandigarh just rang a bell. Fabio Fibmaster was born and brought up in Chandigarh. It was too preliminary to correlate but I strongly thought that this evening itself I might end up hearing some interesting stories about Yuvraj Singh.

Fabio came back from office with a bounce in his gait and cheeky smile; within no time he announced his immense happiness to us.

"I am so happy for Yuvraj, he totally deserves it," remarked Fabio.

"I am sure he does. He has had a good run to get selected," I replied.

"I knew long back that he would play for India. We have played some inter college tournaments together," continued Fabio.

"Oh I didn't know that. In fact, I didn't even know that you played cricket," I replied with a bit surprise.

"You will never believe what I am going to tell you," urged Fabio

"How many times do I have to tell you that I can believe anything," I chipped in

"It was an inter college tournament. I started my first over and I must tell you that I had quite a good reputation as a fast bowler. My first ball which to my mind was not short enough was pulled for a six. It was for the first time ever in my life that my first ball was hit for a six. I charged back and bowled a beautiful out swinger, but the batsman went on the backfoot and drove it past the covers gloriously for a four. I had never seen anything like this before. I just could not resist asking the umpire who the player was. And when the umpire told me his name, I knew that Yuvraj Singh was special and one day he would play for India. I am so happy my thinking has come true," Fabio went on with his fictitious fable.

"Fabio, you are fabulous. So you go battered as a bowler at the hands of Yuvraj Singh." I teased him a little

"Hang on! You have not heard the full story yet. The third ball was a superfast in-swinging yorker. Before Yuvraj Singh could lift his bat, the bails were seen flying in the sky. Clean bowled!" said he with pride

"I had to leave cricket when I joined engineering. In fact, Yuvraj requested me so much to continue playing cricket. He felt I was the fast bowler that India has been looking for since 1947."

"Then you are a fool you didn't continue playing cricket," I said.

"I had promised my dad that I would be an engineer. I can break anything, except my promises," Fabio found some lame excuse.

"You can still try, you are just 25," I challenged him.

"I had a terrible knee injury two years back, my cricketing days are over. Besides, I love being a software engineer." He came up with some more arguments.

"Anyways, cricket or no cricket I am looking forward to partying with Yuvraj Singh when Indian cricket team plays its match in Mumbai any time soon,'" I tried to corner him.

"There is a small reality beyond what I told you. During one of the university matches when my team defeated Yuvraj's team, we had a major tiff off the ground and we have not spoken ever since. The misunderstanding could never be sorted out. But nevertheless, he is indeed the best player I have ever seen and I am sure he will do India proud.

"Someday I am sure our misunderstanding will be sorted and we will be friends again," he quipped putting an end to his cock and bull story.

And yes, Yuvraj has definitely done India proud; I just realized one more importance of circa 2000. Yuvraj Singh made his fantastic debut (referring to his first innings which I think came in the second match of the series) with a majestic 80 odd runs against mighty Australia and who can forget the stellar role he played in winning us the World Cup in 2011!

But Yuvraj Singh probably does not know that he has known and even fought with Fabio Fibmaster.

Bogus Bond

There are different types of deadly combinations in this world; fire and fuel is one of them for instance, so was the combination of Ronaldo and Ronaldinho, when they played soccer together for Brazil. Mediocrity and 'I am the best' attitude is also an extremely lethal combination if we extend this logic to human behaviour. He believed (with oodles of misconception) that he was far more rocking than James Bond; while in reality he was not even a vagabond. But either ways, he happens to be our new character so we will call him '*Bogus Bond*'.

Hailing from a family of super achievers with their achievements varying from 'above average to awesome', he was the odd man out. His father was a hot shot entrepreneur and a proven achiever owning about half a dozen enterprises in Dehradun, a couple of resorts around the valley and an extremely popular playschool that was blooming under the supervision of his socialite mother. Mamma Bond was a high flying society woman having won a few highly insignificant beauty pageants, such as "College Queen", "Mrs. Christmas Ball" (in a club where her husband was the trustee and the founder). Nevertheless, her living room displayed the beauty crowns accompanied by photographs with her mouth half open - eyes half closed and hands on the cheeks oozing an expression, "Oh my god, I can't believe that I have won this title too". The school was a fantastic platform for her to project a 'beauty with purpose' kind of branding in the city. It is a different matter that if Papa Bond allowed her to change the name of the playschool, she would have surely it as "Page 3 playschool"

His elder brother was a rockstar in the metaphoric as well as literal sense. Excellent in academics and more than rocking with the guitar, he had inherited the good looks from his mother and had the suave mannerisms of his father. Needless to say, he was a rage among the youth. It can be called sheer irony or simply the balancing act of nature that Bogus Bond was exactly the opposite of his entire family, but his problem was that he was not aware of this at all. He thought he was a more precious commodity than Uranium and God's ultimate gift to mankind. Through another analogy, Bond felt that he was more important to the girls of Dehradun than even River Nile for the people of Egypt.

Bogus Bond was a mediocre student, short in height, but made up the height deficiency with his weight. He was darker with a saggy body language and a funny pseudo American English accent. To make matters worse, he had a persistent medical problem in his toes due to which he was advised by doctors not to wear shoes; instead he was recommended loose slippers. The problem of course eventually got resolved in a year's time, but it ruined his image during his flamingly youthful teenage days as a very un-cool guy and he got the nickname *"Slipperman"* from his classmates when he would have ideally dreamt of being called *Superman*. Beautiful girls of Dehradun were naturally not interested in a *'Slipperman'*.

The problem with Bond was that he thought he had good looks of Tom Cruise, genius of Newton, the sensitivity of Oprah Winfrey (cannot think of any man immediately), style of George Clooney and, of course, the inherited money of his father. Of the entire list, only thing that he really had was the money. And we all know that there are some things which money can't buy. However, it was a very interesting theory that I discovered with Bogus Bond flaunting his fat wallet to every possible eligible girl. I realized there are some guys "who are only good enough to pay restaurant bills" and in turn paying restaurant bills had no direct correlation in winning the heart of a girl. This led to discovery of "Law of paying restaurant bills" and you will find loads of men who fall into this category.

Every girl has a vision of 'prince charming' who is the most perfect man in the universe because he is rich, princely, stylish, handsome, intelligent, understanding, monogamous, humorous, sporty, macho and yet sensitive. In fact he is the most fictitious man who never exists in reality. Likewise every man has a mental image of a 'princess charming' who has intelligence, most gorgeous possible looks, most heavenly curves, great understanding, who never pesters or follows up for anything, has the highest degree of patience and never ever loses her cool, whatever the situation might be. This princess charming surely does not exist on planet earth. Likewise Bogus Bond had similar misconceptions about himself and to him he was the ultimate "Self Charming".

Special Features and Tendencies:
* Brand ambassador of iconic mirages.

- Wholesale trader of illusions and hallucinations.
- Had a pseudo accent which ranged gloriously from American to Australian including European depending upon the situation.

The truth remains that he was not even mediocre. Bond had more misconceptions about himself than the entire total of crude oil reserves in the world.

Incidentally, our families were well known to each other on a social level and this caused a great deal of stress for me, as he would unnecessarily pile on to me and I had to always entertain him for a wee bit (out of sheer courtesy) till I could excuse myself from the perilous situation. Apart from being in the same institute, we were also in the same coaching class for engineering admissions, thus making it a double blow for me. He perceived me as a friend of last resort. Unfortunately, he did not have many friends, so invariably his last resort was most often his first resort. To me, he was the metaphor of a glue stick with radioactive properties as he would overtly try to hang around with me causing extremely irritating radiations.

Bogus Bond had several illusions about his self-perceived "self charming" sketch. So you can well imagine what would happen when a highly seasoned teenager (about 18 at that time) with such humungous illusions falls in love for the first time.

The hallucinations are severe and they will unfold in the next story.

> **If you ever meet him**: Please allow him to pay the restaurant bills; that's the only expertise that he has.

Bogus Bond and mystery of the outsourced brother

Engineers usually fall in love with logic, calculations, machines and mechanisms. Their passion to love these things is globally accepted and acknowledged. It takes much more effort for engineers to ignore the above and fall in love with a real woman. But if that happens, there is bound to be an explosion you cannot ignore. Bogus Bond was not yet an engineer but he was preparing for engineering entrance exams. And yes, a powerful explosion took place even before he could join engineering.

Every thing about the engineering coaching was terribly stuffing and suffocating except a fresh breeze which would flow in with the batch next to ours. The fresh breeze was Miss Riya Madaan and she was enrolled in the 5–7 p.m. batch, while we struggled our way in the 3–5 p.m. slot. I have never been able to understand the reason why she wanted to get into engineering. She was like a perfect model material; it was just a matter of time when she would sign a contract with any well-known modelling agency. Why was engineering on her radar? I really don't know, however, if she ever got into an engineering college, there would be a sure shot riot because of her. By temperament and overall cosmic consciousness, engineering colleges are not designed to accommodate such deadly beauties.

Yes, she resembled a Hollywood star when she wore her dark glasses adding to her natural style and appeal. Yes, she was exactly the woman that could challenge the beauty of Lord Byron's inspiration in his famous poem "She Walks in Beauty". Yes, she was probably the prettiest women I had come across in my life. Please don't get me wrong; this is not my love story.

Every rational person understands the difference between window shopping and actual splurging. I have spent enough man hours in my life admiring the expensive watches of Audemars Piguet and Vacheron Constantin through the glass window; but it has never got converted into an obsession to buy them. Yes, aspirational value is important for long term growth, but it cannot be allowed to become short term foolhardiness. In an analogical manner, I have never been able to understand how some men fall in love with the prettiest possible women without having ever spoken to them. It is fine to like and admire from a distance, but falling in "one sided" love is weird. Bond met with a similar fate when he fell in love with Riya Madaan after merely seeing her on a few occasions.

"I think she is the girl I have been waiting for! She is my dream woman and I think I can't resist making her my girlfriend," Bond announced his intentions, loud and clear.

"You are right. I have exactly the same sentiments for her. Although my sentiments are far milder and inconsequential, I believe most men can develop these feelings for a woman who is outwardly so attractive," I replied.

"What are you hinting at?" Bond sounded a bit miffed.

"I am not hinting at anything. Just take it easy and give it some more time to settle down. It may be a high level of infatuation which may mellow down with time." I was trying to be a reasonable counsellor.

"You are trying to divert my attention and are jealous of me," snapped Bond

"What is there to be jealous of? You may fall in love with Buckingham Palace, but it will still continue to belong to the Queen. I see no difference in the situation; she does not even know your name and you are making castles in the air," I retorted.

"Yes my friend, castles are already made, now I just need to bring them down to the ground. Just wait for my charm to work and very soon she will be inside my castle while you will be the one running around my castle to catch a glimpse of her," replied the overconfident Bogus Bond.

"You are too much. How do you define your charm?" I asked.

"Something like James Bond; may be a little more than his. He is better than me in action and I am probably better in romance," replied Bond.

"Unbelievable! But on seconds thoughts, fools like you are needed on the earth to balance out the sanity," I replied.

"You called me a fool? Just wait and watch how I move the earth beneath her feet and then she will need my arms for finding her balance," Bond went on and on.

"She is the chosen one and indeed cosmic grace is on her side as she is the lucky girl for whom I have developed my first ever crush," Bond was unstoppable.

Beliefs are funny things, they need not have any link with

reality. Centuries ago, humans believed that sun went around the earth till it was proven otherwise. Likewise, Bond also had the belief that he was a charming sun around whom the girls were dying to hover.

Bogus Bond was definitely not amongst my best friends. He was just a normal acquaintance. In today's perspective, we all have many friends who are just connected to us because of Facebook. Other than that, chances of staying connected would be slim. In spite of this, I tried my best to counsel him like I would do to my best friend. When all the counselling and persuading failed to work, I distanced myself and became a spectator of the stupid things waiting to take place.

A couple of friends from the coaching class – Sandy and Richa – sensed Bond's boiling hot infatuation for Riya. In fact, his infatuation and conduct was so obvious that even a blind person would be able to see that. Sandy and Richa thought he was a fool of the highest pedigree and it is only very natural to have some fun at his expense.

One evening after we came out of the class, both of them took him aside and provoked him to behave in a manner in keeping with his infatuation.

"I have never seen a bigger coward than you. When you like her so much, why don't you let her know," Sandy announced.

"Hey! I will. I am just waiting for her to see enough of me and develop some familiarity with me. My charm will work shortly," replied Bond with his fake and deep rooted 'self charming' coolness.

"India is an overpopulated country; you should never waste even a single day to book your train tickets or to convey your feelings to a girl. It may be too late to discover that all the seats are already reserved," added Richa playing a mind trick on Bond.

"You never know, she might have a boyfriend or god forbid there may be someone else also vying for a chance," Sandy made matters more explicit.

"Thanks Richa and Sandy; you have brought in a much needed urgency. There will be a grand expression of love very soon." Bond thanked them for showing this new dimension and hastened away from the tuitions.

The die had been cast and the dice had been rolled. A fool was ready to conquer the universe. His ambition could have put Alexander to shame.

The next day Bond came in his father's car with a massive gift hamper placed on the back seat. The gift hamper looked like "half a boutique" to me. "These are some of the privileges of such a rich father," I thought to myself.

As we came out of our tuitions, the next batch including Riya was waiting outside. Bond was a man in a hurry; he quickly introduced himself to Riya.

"Hi. The name is Bond," he announced with a beaming smile.

"I don't care if you are Bond or Indiana Jones. What do you want?" she replied.

"Two minutes of yours if you could come out of the premises," he requested.

She looked disgusted and appeared equally concerned being surrounded by co-students while this drama was unfolding.

"Quickly," she made her stance clear.

Bond leaped out like a frog and brought the hamper from the car along with a gigantic card.

"I have adored you from a distance. I want to extend my

friendship to you. Please accept this hamper and card as a gesture of friendship." Bond mildly proposed the congenial arrangement of friendship to begin with.

"Are you crazy? I don't even know who you are," she tore the card and refused the hamper.

We all knew that she was piping hot but I discovered that day that she was fiery too.

"Just get lost and don't try this stunt ever again," Riya was fuming and firm.

Like a fierce wind, she opened the door and went back into the class.

The cyclone had come and gone; all that remained outside was some torn pieces of the card, an untouched gift hamper and a devastated Bond.

"It is okay. Very often it begins with a friction," Richa consoled Bond.

"Yes. But she is made of a sword," said Bond.

"Let us call her Helen of Troy," added Sandy just wanting to change the mood.

Bond took a deep breath and said, "I will not give up. The charm will surely work."

I was amazed at his sense of optimism and high coefficient of illusion. In the next few days, Bond tried several trivial tricks such as:

- Attempting to talk again and again.
- Blocking her way to the class.
- Celebrating false birthdays to invite her to his self invented birthday parties.
- Sending love letters through little boys and girls of the neighborhood.

Bond was all over the place, had clearly lost his sanity and went on for 2 weeks with his unruly ways. He had become an idiotic stalker. He was not dangerous but utterly foolish in his conduct. Sandy and Richa kept motivating Bond not to give up the chase and he kept relying on his "charming" persona and false assurances from Richa and Sandy.

Girls have a good sixth sense and probably Riya had discovered he was a harmless buffoon being played upon by his friends. However, she never gave even a decimal of a bit to his advances. I feared that she would soon give up and complain to police or her parents or the coaching class.

Riya also had the sense that some of us were actually pushing Bond to do these stupidities. While Richa and Sandy were indeed having fun at his expense, I was not involved in any form of provocation. Each time our batch left and her batch entered the tutorials,' Riya used to give us a dirty look which clearly said, "You jerks stop pushing and provoking Bond to do what he is doing."

I was not provoking him and was not at all comfortable with the idea that one of the "most eligible girls of Dehradun" perceived me as a manipulator.

One of the evenings I returned home after the tutorials and found a visitor at home. She was Rita Aunty who happened to be a part of my mother's "cards and kitty circle". I had known this classy high society lady for a long time as my mother often met her in clubs, social gatherings and of course while playing cards. However, I had never ever met her family.

"Good evening aunty," I greeted her with a pleasing smile.

"Good evening. So how are you doing and which stream are you planning to pursue in college?" she asked.

"I am preparing for engineering entrance," I replied to her.

"Are you attending any tutorial?" she inquired.

"Yes. I go to Professor Singh," I replied.

"He is the best. Which batch are you in?" She questioned me further.

"I am in the 3 to 5 batch," I said.

"Are you in the 3 to 5 batch?" she did not seem to like that at all. I could not really figure out why but she did not like the fact that I was in '3 to 5' batch. The whole facial expression probably meant that '3 to 5' is a batch of goons.

"Anyways my daughter also goes to Professor Singh. She is in the 5 to 7 batch," she said arousing my worst fears.

The whole story was now falling in place in my mind.

"What is your daughter's name?" I asked with mild suspicion and fear.

"Riya Madaan," she threw a bombshell at me.

"Oh God, yet another example of a small world," I thought to myself.

I sincerely hoped that she did not bring up any topic about the rogue behaviour that her daughter was witnessing in the 3 to 5 batch. She was a classy lady and left our house without hinting at that.

The next day when I reached the tutorials, I told Richa and Sandy to stop this melodrama as Riya had turned out to be a family friend. I was worried about my wrong impression in my mother's social circle and my poor mother had no clue about that. They understood the situation and promised full co-operation in bringing down the addiction levels of the lover boy.

As luck would have it, Rita aunty came to drop Riya to

tutorials that day. She had probably come to give Bond and us a piece of her mind. Incidentally, Bond was absent that day.

"Hi Aunty," I wished her sheepishly.

"Hi. I am sure you know Riya," she said in a matter of fact tone.

"I don't know her, just familiar," I replied shamefacedly.

"But your friend wants to know her. Correct?" Rita aunty sounded aggressive.

"I don't know much about it," I replied awkwardly.

"Stop acting ignorant," she replied.

Riya called out to Richa and Sandy to complete the loop in one attempt.

"Please tell your friend to stop this nonsense otherwise I will complaint to Professor Singh," Riya made her point clear.

"You are like my son, so please sort this out," Rita aunty made her demand clear and she left.

It seemed like a threat to me.

The next day we called Bond over to a coffee shop.

"When are you stopping this nonsense?" I asked Bond firmly.

"What nonsense?" Bond inquired.

"Chasing Riya," I replied.

"I cannot stop that. Man, I love her," Bond seemed to be still gung ho despite three weeks of rejection.

"The charm will work someday," he added.

"It has not worked so far and being a woman, I have a sense that it will not work," Richa chipped in.

"There are no discussions in this. I will win her someday," Bond persisted.

We tried really hard but the negotiations failed. Bond was too adamant and persistent. No matter how much we tried, the man was unshakable.

The angry Bond left the coffee halfway and darted out of the café.

"Now what?" questioned Richa.

"Rocky," I replied.

"Who Rocky?" asked Sandy.

"Rocky Thapa," I replied.

Rocky Thapa was a local college goon more popularly known as Thapa. He had quite a notorious reputation. I happened to know him through a friend from my neighborhood who was in youth politics.

If Riya was white as curd, Rocky was blacker than coal.

If Riya looked like heaven, Rocky looked like hell.

If Riya was like a graceful swan, Rocky was a dangerous cobra.

I got hold of my neighbor and sought his help to sort this matter. The plan was to project Rocky as the brother of Riya and threaten Bond with dire consequences. Rocky had a tarnished reputation and was well-known amongst students.

Rocky Thapa agreed to play the role of her brother.

"Rocky. You have only to threaten. No hitting or pushing please," I requested.

"Not even little? Some amount of force makes good impact," suggested Rocky.

"Let us do it the Mahatma Gandhi style. No violence please," I pleaded.

"As you wish," replied Rocky.

"We will see you tomorrow at 3," I thanked Rocky and my neighbor Ajit for organizing the meeting with Rocky.

Bond reached at 3. Rocky was waiting for him. So was I.

"Are you Bond?" Rocky grabbed him by his collar.

Bond was trembling as he knew Rocky was a hooligan.

"Yes. But why?" replied a shivering Bond.

"Why don't you become my friend and leave my sister alone? How dare you bother Riya?" Rocky pounced on Bond.

"I am sorry. Your sister is my sister," replied a half fainting Bond, in a jiffy changing his stance from a lover to a half brother.

Then Rocky had this rush of blood and he gave some tight slaps to Bond on both sides of his face.

"Bang Bang/ Boom Boom!"

Rocky and his gang exited after the flurry of blows. This was not a part of the plan, but nevertheless, it happened. I never ever mustered courage to ask Rocky why did he go beyond his brief.

"Are you okay, Bond?" I asked him.

"No. Head is spinning. The jaw is paining," replied a shocked Bond.

"And the eye is swollen," I added.

We took Bond to the doctor to get him the necessary first aid and medical attention.

While we were walking out of the doctor's clinic, Bond uttered some words finally after a long spell of silence.

"I still cannot figure out how a pretty girl like Riya and ugly man like Rocky be brother and sister."

"Don't worry. Anything is possible. 'R' for Riya and 'R' for Rocky. I can see some connection," I replied.

The matter ended there. Rita aunty got a son called Rocky and Riya got a brother and a formal apology from my side. Bond is still not convinced and his brotherhood is still a mystery to him. However, he has never looked straight at Riya from that day.

And yes, my mother still does not know about it.

Jargon Smith

In my very own personal opinion, Google has been the best invention of the 21st century. Larry Page has indeed gone beyond the paradigm of business and has reached an extent of causing extremely significant social impact on the lives of people. It is quite possible that in the future, the psychologists while analyzing the human behaviour or learning mechanisms, may prefer a pre-Google or post-Google division to demonstrate the changing dynamics of human learning better through power of information.

If Larry Page is a high inventor (and innovator), Jargon Smith is a high user. Jargon Smith had a core belief in life "Except your mother and father, you can find everything else through Google."

"You can find a job;

You can even find a wife," he would often say.

I have the highest regard for Google and it is by default my homepage when I launch Internet. It is indeed changing the face of information management (amongst many other things) in this era of technology.

In this particular case, Google was a great tool in hands of a hollow man. Jargon Smith was indeed very hollow, very shallow and a highly myopic person. He was too much in love with periphery to have ever tried to reach a center of anything.

And based on his beliefs, he had formed some basic principles of existence on which he faked his entire outward life.

The first principle was the "Law of AAGI".

"When you feel that you know nothing, remember there are millions of jargons left to flaunt your knowledge. And these millions of jargons can be explored by a click of a button. This technique of jargon acquisition is called 'Artificially acquired Google Intellect' (AAGI) and this was his first law of existence."

Jargon Smith would pretend to be taking urgent calls or messages in middle of certain meetings, while my guess is that he used this valuable time to search some buzz words through Internet. Once these buzz words and jargons were in his control, then you could see him getting more offensive by liberally throwing some of newly acquired intellect.

The second principle was the "Law of motherhood statements".

Jargon Smith derived a high degree of kick by being vague. He used high level of truth to get away with the lower level granularities which he did not know. While the truth was correct in its own way, it was not useful in most organizational situations.

For example, if I say that "Earth is a blue planet", the statement is absolutely correct. However, I am not sure how much this one line will help a student appearing for a geography examination. He will still need to know the capital of Cameroon if the question paper asks for it.

Jargon Smith strived and thrived on excessive usage of "motherhood statements". If you asked him specific risks in a particular project, his reply would be:

"My worry is very different. Overall fiscal deficit is a matter of great concern. The situation in Europe is tense and I am worried about the double dip recession. To take an isolated view in such a scenario is very difficult for me. The world is truly becoming flat and we had better respect this fact."

The reply obviously has no semblance of the project being discussed.

The third Principle was the Law of Scientific Nomenclature.

Smith had the unique knack of complicating simple things into complex situations. He used various tools such as scientific nomenclatures and technical rubbish to create the desired effect.

Smith could stump a little kid by asking him to pass Sodium Chloride at a dinner table, till someone else would ask the little child to not think so much and simply pass on the salt. For him, sunflower was *Helianthus*, an earthworm was *Lumbricus Terrestris* and a domestic dog was *Canis lupus familaris* going as per their Botanical and Zoological names, respectively. Human beings by that same rationale would be *Homo Sapiens* and you could probably understand why Jargon Smith was one of the rare breed himself.

This law created a unique pseudo firewall for allowing people to show their superiority.

The fourth and foremost "Law of buying time."

For the first three laws to work, there is one big dependency. And it is not difficult to guess. Yes, all that Jargon Smith ever needed was time in solitude to gather the ammunition required to deflect or redirect or jeopardize the discussion. If breathing is the most important activity to stay alive, then acquiring pseudo knowledge through Internet is the most important activity to stay afloat at work.

The fourth law came in handy. Jargon Smith would always buy time so that he could come prepared with his bagful of jargon, motherhood statements and scientific props.

His typical response for a fresh invite would be:

"No time to breathe buddy; how about discussing this after two days?"

His typical response to a situation while in middle of a meeting would be:

"I am so sorry, but you have to excuse me for ten minutes. One urgent transaction needs immediate attention. Please carry on with the discussion I will join you in ten minutes."

Jargon Smith was indeed a unique character. He had scaled new heights of pseudoism and I believe such rare heights can be reached only by a spaceship. It is difficult for any other *Homo sapiens* to reach that altitude. However, I am sure all of us have mini Jargon Smiths all around us and can relate to his laws of existence.

Special features and tendencies:
- King of jargons.
- He was a management pilot as all his statements were at 60,000 feet level and had no correlation to ground reality.
- Was all gas and no meat.

If you ever find him:
1. Get specific and cut the crap.
2. Keep the agenda well defined in advance.
3. Lock the door from outside and snatch his phone;
   enjoy him at barest best for a change.

Taj Mahal and the glory of Calcium Carbonate

Jargon Smith was a wholesale trader of jargons. Just try to imagine what kind of sparks would fly if this highly evolved jargonizer even ran into a man who was very obsessed with trivial facts of life. On one side we have a person who cannot get to facts and on the other, we have a person who is too frozen with facts that do not matter. Well, there is no need to imagine. It actually happened.

An eminent European dignitary had once visited our office to give us some unwanted dope (which the management obviously thought was important) on leadership effectiveness and styles. He was a professor in a reputed university and had devoted his entire life towards giving 'blah blah' lectures on the topic of leadership. For the sake of convenience and also for concealing his real identity, let us call him Professor John Johnny John.

Speaking from the gut and not by facts, I feel that Taj Mahal and Indian IT industry attracts maximum foreign visitors to India. On closer examination of John Johnny John, I found that more than 'Blah Blah' sessions he was more interested in visiting the Taj Mahal while he was in India. Johnny was supposed to John around (read John as Fuck) for nearly two weeks in our company in order to meet various levels of managers and ensure that he got a chance to torture the maximum possible souls in our organization. When things get bad, they can really get nasty. During one of the weekends, our organization had organized a trip to Taj Mahal for John Johnny John as an extended courtesy. To make matters more complicated, I was assigned the task of escorting him. And now coming to the nasty part, our friend Jargon Smith had also been asked to join us for the visit as a representative from the senior management.

John was a strict theoretician, while Smith was a certified jargon factory and I was a poor victim who was stuck between the devil and the deep sea. I had recently acquired a girl friend after very strategic wooing and overcoming a very stiff competition. Leaving my 'dolly bird' back in Mumbai, I was sandwiched between a fuddy-duddy professor and a dodgy podgy Jargon Smith.

The three musketeers had taken a taxi from Delhi to Agra. While in the taxi the professor was quick to display his fascination for meaningless facts:

"Mumtaz was indeed a lucky woman for whom this great symbol of love was made. But I see a big disconnect. Mumtaz was spelt as M …U … M …T… A....Z; so why is it not called Taz Mahal instead of Taj Mahal?" Professor opened a can of theoretical worms.

Jargon Smith is normally impotent without Google but he still had "Law of Motherhood" statements to bail him out.

"You have made an interesting point. I think the Moguls did not know good English and the British did not know good

Persian. Spelling might have got sacrificed in the knowledge gap," replied Jargon.

"Ah. What a fantastic thought. Many companies have been doomed in this knowledge gap. The knowledge gap, however small, is always wide enough to cause severe damage," replied the leadership superman.

"Mumtaz was Shahjahan's third wife. So can we say he was 'third time lucky' in love?" Professor John Johnny John went on with his theoretical masturbation.

"He was lucky to have a third wife. Usually all possibilities exhaust with the first one in the lives of lesser mortals," replied Smith with seemingly personal feelings attached.

The nonsensical conversations went on throughout the three hour drive. Anyway, we reached Agra and I was extremely happy to step out of the taxi to get the fresh breath of air.

While the two of us (the professor and I) were clearly enamored by the breathtaking beauty of Taj Mahal, it was apparent that Jargon Smith was on a different trip. Before I could figure out the reason, Smith went high with the "law of scientific nomenclatures". As it turned out, I felt that I was not in one of the modern wonders of the world, but rather in a chemical laboratory.

"Calcium Carbonate is the most amazing chemical compound," said Smith.

"Yeah, must be, but why are you thinking of it in front of Taj Mahal?" I replied

"Calcium carbonate is found in chalk, in limestone, in arogonite and even in marble. I think it is nature's deep rooted philosophy that with the same ingredient, it can produce minerals and rocks which look so different from each other.

It is the same calcium carbonate which makes Taj Mahal look so beautiful, built from the best quality marble of the world." Jargon Smith got more scientific and passionate about calcium carbonate.

"Well, with or without Calcium Carbonate, it is a magnificent structure," I tried to downplay the jargon.

"Do you know calcium carbonate forms about 4% of the earths crust?" he was still carbonating.

"No, I didn't know that, but by that logic, there should have been more Taj Mahals in the world. I think it is human ambition and a dream to seek perfection which creates such wonders, otherwise there would be little Taj Mahals outside every lime stone quarry," I replied.

"There is no doubt that artisans have done a good job but you cannot take the credit away from Calcium Carbonate," Jargon Smith got stuck with obsession.

"I never thought on these lines. You have made me realize the glory of calcium carbonate," suddenly Smith found a supporter in form of John Johnny John.

"It is not uncommon to find two brothers given the same upbringing grow into two different individuals, one could be a successful upright guy and other turn out a manipulating loser. It is the same calcium carbonate which goes into their value system but the final product is as different as chalk and stone," Professor was hooked on to the idea.

"I will conduct a detailed research on the dependence on input factors on eventual success of human beings and mind you Smith, I will dedicate the research to the glory of calcium carbonate," John sealed the topic.

Section 4

Titbits

This book is about everyday humour, funny tendencies and light stories that keep mushrooming around all of us. The book is based on the principle of simple observations and derives juice out of mundane situations of day-to-day living. Not all observations are large enough to be made a character or become full-fledged anecdotes. There are many random moments which are funny and worth describing. The last section is appropriately named Titbits and contains random observations pertaining to "words people use" and "peculiar behaviours" that people demonstrate in some situations.

Section A– Based on Words
Section B– Based on Behaviour

Chapter 13

Titbits and Everyday Humour

Part A– Changing Words with Changing Times
Oh Fish 1

Oh fish is nothing but "Oh fuck when seen through a veil". The user of language, when he wishes to convey sentiments related to the word 'Fuck' but feels the intense need of censorship due to surrounding environment, resorts politely to the word 'fish' as a modest substitute. But here the listener has to be very considerate and equate the feelings associated with the word 'fuck.'

The days are gone when fish were only meant to be eaten; now they are also meant to be spoken.

Deck

The word deck is no ordinary word. The increasing number of applications of this word stands as a testimony to human spirit for progress. From being referred initially to the floor of a ship, the word deck got transformed into a pack of cards. The evolution did not end there and the word deck began to be used as a slang for music / sound reproduction system. This word got a shot in the arm when phrases such a 'hit the deck' became an informal means for conveying a fall on to the ground. Entering into the 21st century, the word deck is now being increasingly used by management consultants to describe a power point presentation or some strategic reports.

In the future, the word 'deck' holds tremendous promise to find newer applications.

Taking a call

In the 20th century 'taking a call' was a prestigious thing as not too many people had telephones that time. With rampant mobile telephony that exists these days, taking a call is no longer prestigious from the telecommunications stand point. Hence, a sweeping innovation was needed to bring these words back to their original glory. Therefore, in the 21st century context, 'taking a call' has gone through a revolutionary and a radical change. The word 'decision-making' is slowly fading away as the new culture of 'decision-making' is getting shadowed under the phenomenon of 'taking a call'. By equating decision-making with 'taking a call', the lost prestige of these words are back in the reckoning.

Cool

The word 'cool' is like a well-diversified conglomerate with many subsidiaries. 'Cool' is also like a rainbow in the sky. It has many colors and many strategic uses. Gone are the days when cool was used to denote the concept of 'cold' or 'phenomenon pertaining to lower temperatures'. Now cool has become a part of daily life with host of varied uses.

Cool can mean okay.

Cool can mean suave and charming.

Cool can mean easygoing.

Cool can also be a supplementary word to add more respect to the humble word 'ok'.

Cool can continue to denote lower temperatures and pleasant weathers.

The coolness of the word cool has been contagious. Now the word 'Chill' (it is like a subsidiary of cool) has also become fairly multifaceted and can be used in contexts such as 'relaxing' or 'having a good time.'

Screw

The word 'screw' has been an incredible all-rounder like the word fuck. Robust and versatile, the word 'screw' has been a chartbuster in the English language. From traditionally being a type of nut /fastener characterized by helical ridges or simply external threads with an ability to be tightened by rotation, it has evolved into a highly metaphorical word to describe awkward situations. The modern use of the word 'screw' comes with an amazing degree of calibration depending upon the tone, diction and intensity of the speaker.

Screwed could mean getting mildly scolded, going up to being fired indiscriminately.

Screwed could also mean an intercourse (chances of this intercourse having the purity of love making is less).

Screwed could also mean making a complete mess of a particular situation.

Tightening the screw is often informally used to describe

the scenario of squeezing resources to make life difficult for someone.

The word screw also continues to describe nuts, bolts and fasteners as per its original connotation.

One can now literally screw around with the word 'screw'.

Rock

The word rock has seen exponential prosperity is the last few decades. From originally being a part of the geology world, it made a grand entry into the world of music in the 1960s. From scientific types such as igneous, sedimentary and metamorphic, it got added dimensions such as soft rock or hard rock depending upon the dominance of bass guitar and drums.

The word rock then made way for its close cousins such as rockstar and the word 'rocking'. In fact, the word 'rocking' itself has gone through a paradigm shift. From originally used to denote some sort of movement, it has now become a symbol for 'good times'.

Likewise, the word rock can continue to mean rock.

Rock can also mean to have a great time.

Rock can be used to describe high energy situations.

Rockstar can be a musical genius.

Rockstar can also be a confident cool dude.

The other related phrases such as 'rock on' add more charm to the evergreen beauty of this rock.

While diamonds might still be precious, it is the broad based utility of the word 'rock' that has captured the imagination of Queen's English.

Chick

As per the original English language, the word chick was used to represent a baby chicken or even generically used to describe small birds that have not reached the adult stage. There has been a drastic swing in its application from the bird kingdom to the world of humans. Now the word 'chick' is being increasingly used to describe an attractive and sexy young woman.

Boy, oh Boy!

Yes, you would have read the word boy two times. But the matter of fact is that it has nothing to do with a boy or a girl or rather any part of human sexuality. 'Boy, oh boy!' has been a unique invention which tends to convey the emotions of the speaker. The emotions could be happy, sad or even filled with surprise. It fits in beautifully to describe different types of feelings.

Boy oh boy, I forgot to send the email. Now my boss is going to screw me.

I went to the airport on Sunday morning to pick my mother up and boy oh boy I saw Tom Cruise walking out of the arrival hall.

Analyze this: *Boy oh boy, the chick was really cool.*

If this line was read by your grandfather at the time of Indian Independence, he would interpret that someone is talking to a boy about a freezing cold chicken and chances were that he would strongly advocate the need of well-cooked chicken instead of eating it raw and cold.

When you read through today's lingo, you realize that this line has nothing to do with a boy or a chicken or cold temperature. Rather, this line describes an attractive girl.

Wassup

Just like Egypt is the gift of the Nile, Wassup is the gift of chat software's and SMS technology. Wassup is merger and amalgamation of 'what's up?' And this merger has nothing to do with what is really up.

Our grandfathers would typically reply roof or sky or even God as a matter of fact answer to this question. However, now this has become a cooler way to ask 'how you are.'

The word Wassup is also becoming a license to flirt mildly or open dialogue through SMSs or on chat sites.

Part B – Peculiar Behaviours

Shaking Hands syndrome

From eons, shaking hands has been a gesture of introduction and greeting one another. While the gesture still holds its meaning, there are few people who cannot differentiate where the gesture stops and possession starts. This is the category of people who do not leave your hand easily when offered for a customary handshake. They probably believe that once a hand is offered for handshake, it is legally transferred in their name and hence there is no need to leave it. It now belongs to them and now they can take it home. No, they are not gays or lesbians, but generally have a tendency to linger on with your hands without any material gain to anyone. And needless to say, it's quite irritating.

Facebook Access Syndrome

Facebook is a rage and deservedly so, but I have seen that most of the dormant users suddenly become active when they reach an airport or more significantly when they reach a foreign location. There are some changes that take place in hormones and inner chemistry that upon reaching a foreign location they instantly update their status with a tiny little "In Bangkok" or "In Singapore" to broadcast an additional stamping on their passport. In fact, I recall someone updating his status three times in the same week saying the same thing, "In Sydney for a week," which I thought was obviously overdoing it unless he had reached the planet Mercury and was expressing his surprise to have withstood the high temperatures for the entire week.

"Know it all" syndrome (or 'Reprimanding Vatsyayana' syndrome)

Few people have this in abundance. They have some supernatural power to intercept what is in your mind. There are few bosses who know everything in the universe and even better than the inventors themselves. I had one such boss. Hypothetically, if he ever met Vatsyayana (the one who wrote *Kamasutra*), I am sure he would reprimand him for some twenty odd positions that he did not envisage. If I ever went with a problem to him, even before I could finish, he would intercept and confidently say, "I know what you are saying." and "This is what you should do."

Junk Mail Effect

Whenever I read or rather glance at my junk mails, it makes me wonder why the hells do I need to work. As I write this one, I have won two lotteries since yesterday and someone from Africa wants to additionally transfer US$ 1 million to me.

Indian Tourist Syndrome

Thanks to economic developments and booming Indian IT industry, foreign travel has become more common in India. From being a developing economy, now the nomenclature has been upgraded to an emerging market where citizens are now witnessing a fair amount of foreign travel. However, large portion of Indian tourists still make it a point to flaunt their foreign travels to their friends and acquaintances at the first given opportunity. If they do not get an opportunity, they just create one:

"I was in London last month and found the weather awesome."

"The infrastructure sucks in Mumbai, in my last trip to Kuala Lumpur, I was amazed to see their infrastructure." The last trip could have been years back.

"I have been running extremely busy in the last few months. To make matters more tight, I had to make two visits to Singapore last month for some unavoidable work."

"This bar is somewhat like the one I loved in Sydney when I went there last year." I didn't go with him to Sydney and hence cannot refute similarity; however, in the process, I got to know about his trip down under.

The Repetition Syndrome

Some movie channels do not have a large library and hence they go on repeating the same set of movies. There are some people who do not have much to speak about and hence without realizing they keep repeating what they have already said 3 times in 5 minutes. Casual inquiries like 'What's new' and 'What else is happening' never seem to end in a short conversation with them. I knew a middle-aged man in my neighborhood who used to ask me 3 questions every time he met me during my college break vacation in my hometown.

1. When did you come back from college?
2. When are you going back?
3. How is the hostel food?

It was really annoying to answer the same questions again and again. Statistically speaking, I was subjected to this set of questions minimum two times in a week. One fine day I lost my patience, I walked up to him and said on my own:

"Good evening uncle! I came on 5th of this month and going back on 27th of next month. And yes, the hostel food has been consistently pathetic for the last two years."

I think he got the message as I spent the rest of my college life without interrogation.

Self-Disclosure or the IPO syndrome

Just an extension to 'repetition syndrome' comes the anti-thesis known as the self- disclosure syndrome. There are some people who tell you 60% things about their lives in the first meeting and the remaining 40% gets covered in the second meeting. And from the third meeting itself, they start repeating all that they have already told as they have nothing left to say. They remind me of red herring prospectus of corporates which are coming out with Initial public offer (IPO). I know this gentleman who has told me everything about his childhood, to his youth and going right up to his son who works as a trader for an international bank. In fact, I know his son's salary and bonus down to the decimal. And yes, he keeps repeating the entire information pack each time I meet him. Besides how many times he has sex in a week, I know everything about him.

Inquisitive Student Syndrome ('Excessive questioning' syndrome)

While clarifying doubts is a good habit, some people tend to overdo it. There are many people who don't feel sufficiently orgasmic till the time they do not ask a flurry of questions from lecturer or speaker in any other forum for that matter. The most irritating are the ones who start questioning at 1.29 p.m when the lecture is supposed to end at 1.30 p.m and end up overshooting the budget by minimum five minutes. Such students tend to become the famous pests who sabotage most press conferences and investor meetings by their never ending list of questions and counter questions.

"Global Accent of India" syndrome

Indians in general have a unique tendency to adapt to global accents. I have never seen any international visitor adapting or even attempting to adjust to Indian accent while half of the country tends to adapt their accent in a jiffy, trying their best to match them note-by-note. The best incidence I observed was in an airport lounge where one Indian was sandwiched between a Korean and an Englishmen. On the left move, he adapted to Korean accent and on the right, he grappled with the English accent seamlessly. Thankfully, he spoke in a normal accent to the waiter.

Punjabi Mother Syndrome

It is very typical when a boy or a girl gets low scores in school, particularly in North India; his or her mother usually takes off saying that you are an odd lemon out because she used to always come first in the class. And she can't believe how her son or daughter is so mediocre in her comparison.

My mother always came first in her class, so did the mothers of most of my friends in my neighborhood. I really wonder, who came second in their times? Or the full class ended up in a tie on the first spot.

"Professor or knowledge distribution" syndrome

These are the living Wikipedias. They thrive on distributing excess information and can start off like professors at the first given opportunity. If you ever ask them the address of Gateway of India, they will invariably start with its history covering the entire nuance of who built it and why it was built before coming to the detailing of the address.

I suggest that you don't ask them anything; use Google instead.

"60,000 Feet" effect

Live and breathe the strategy, and outsource the execution to teams below. The '60,000 feet effect' represents the large population of managers who thrive and survive on 'Good English, good suits and macro economic bull shit data points'. The whole discourse starts at 60,000 feet level enlightenment talk and stays at that contour forever. Such managers don't discuss specifics and prefer to stay at a really high level. For execution, they blindly trust their teams and their luck. If such a manager has to undertake a project for de-bottlenecking the processes, the only contribution that will come from him will be a sexy name that he will give to a project at the time of kick off, maybe calling it something like a "Mission Fastest". And then leave the remaining to the rest.

The "Secret Romeo" syndrome

Super attractive girls always have plethora of admirers that they are aware of and then they have even larger number of secret admirers that they do not know about. These secret admirers have a tendency to never directly engage with the girls but feed their admiration from back door antics. The secret Romeos have the ridiculous habit of hanging outside their colleges and apartments to catch their glimpse. If by mistake they ever happen to rub their shoulders with hers, then you can expect the Romeo to never wash the shirt that touched the girl. That becomes a 'museum moment' for the secret Romeos and gets preserved forever.

Such admirers have offline parties and celebrations on her birthdays and then eventually get heartbroken when they discover that she has found her real life Romeo.

Life goes on and they find a new crush.

The 'Planning and Gratification' Syndrome

This is a very interesting syndrome, which gets hyper active when you are drinking with close friends. After a few drinks starts the planning phase in which one can plan a road trip to Europe or alternatively plan a jungle safari in South Africa or even go trekking in the Himalayas, or for that matter be the first ones to witness the space tourism whenever it gets started. The planning phase then extends to logistics wherein convenient dates are explored and tentatively fixed before the drinking session gets over. The next day starts afresh whereby the overnight plans are all buried and forgotten till the time you meet your friends again for drinks.

The planning and gratification syndrome is not just limited to travelling, that was just an example. Some people tend to start super specialty restaurants or propose to promote an e-commerce start up. Some psychologists say that loud planning tends to give a false feeling of mild gratification and I think they are right.

The 'General Statements' Syndrome

This syndrome is very common in India. The syndrome hinges on the tendency of making 'general statements' which need not be honoured or considered by the people making them. A typical example would be "let's catch up on the weekend" kind of statement which is usually said to countless number of people while it ends up in meeting none of them. This tendency tends to creep even in office wherein the loose and vague statements such as "let us meet to discuss this in the second half of the day" gets flown around mercilessly. Little do people realize that the second half has four hours and it is too wide a bracket to be left open? If the matter is really urgent, then there is another general statement – 'First thing in morning tomorrow'.

By past experience we also know the second half never comes and neither does that morning.

Indian train passenger syndrome

Indian train travellers have this unique talent of starting conversations with really meaningless topics and then consistently stretching it further to keep the conversation alive.

By the time you get off the train, he would have asked you every possible thing except your bank balance.

If the train is going from Delhi to Mumbai, the conversation pans out something like this:

Passenger: So where are you going?

Victim: Mumbai.

Passenger: So you have some work in Mumbai?

Victim: Yes.

Passenger: That means you actually live in Delhi and are only going to Mumbai for some work. Right?

Victim: Right.

Passenger: I also stay in Delhi. Where do you live in Delhi? I stay at Karol Bagh.

Victim: Greater Kailash.

Passenger: Greater Kailash 1 or 2?

Victim: Greater Kailash 2.

Passenger: Great! My uncle also stays there. His name is Bobbby Brown. He spells his name with 3 B's in the middle. He is a firm believer in numerology. Do you know him?

Victim: No.

Passenger: He is very famous in Greater Kailash 2. Don't worry; I will introduce you to him.

Victim: Thanks.

And it goes on till the victim migrates to the upper berth, pretending to sleep.

"Never drink with your own money" syndrome (or alternatively 'forgotten the wallet' syndrome)

They have all the money in the world to go to Thailand every year and change their gadgets on the day of new launches. Needless to say, they drive long cars and wear fancy watches. But I still don't know what happens to them when they go out for drinks with friends and colleagues. Either they rush to the toilet at the time of billing or their hands get frozen on the way to their pockets or they have simply forgotten to carry their wallet that day. This syndrome is widely popular amongst selected section of friends, family and bosses. Although they keep saying 'I will pay', that never happens. When they return from the toilet they invariably ask you 'why did you pay'?

"Robotic Salesman" syndrome

This syndrome largely pertains to entry level / junior most salesmen which are now often referred to as 'feet on street' in corporate lingo (thankfully managers are not referred as 'shoes on carpet'). Some of them robotically swallow the sales tips and do not digest the intent / spirit of the same. Hence they often turn into script speaking parrots with negligible scope of customizations. I remember, one such 'feet on street' came to my house for a demonstration of some product. As a quick background I had just shifted into this house and it was in a state of total mess. What a normal person considers as messy, I usually classify that as clean. So you can imagine the extent of disaster if I classify something as messy. And let me re-iterate, the house was totally messy due to shifting / furniture scattered everywhere.

Robotic Salesman: "Good afternoon sir."

Me: Good afternoon. Please come inside.

Robotic Salesman: Thank you for letting me in. Sir, I must say that you have such a lovely house.

Me: I have just shifted. It is so messy, what did you find so lovely?

Robotic Salesman: (Not groomed to handle deviations and sporadic questions) Sir, we are trained to say all this. We are given a script in which complimenting a house is mandatory.

This syndrome can be extended to other walks of life. My golfer brother-in-law often tells me that his caddie spontaneously comes up with sounds of 'shot sir' irrespective of how good or bad it may be in reality. The moment the ball leaves the club, the words of appreciation leave from his mouth in perfect synchronicity.

So when you start getting stereotyped replies from some people, you would know that the 'robotic salesman' syndrome is working. Bosses should be particularly alert about this syndrome when they are doing business reviews.

'Love at first sight specialization' syndrome

Strange, but gender tends to play an important role in this syndrome. This syndrome is more prevalent in men. Some men tend to regularly fall in love at first sight, and on careful examination, you will find that they have actually specialized in the art of falling in love. By the time they move from youth to middle age, they would have probably lost count as to how many times have they fallen in love at first sight? These are the specialist's first sight lovers. Our friend Larry Love is one of them.

"Party / Anytime" Syndrome

This is actually a deep rooted transactional analysis syndrome wherein both the persons talking to each other are heavily under the influence of 'general statements' syndrome. The demand for a party or celebrations crops up at the most trivial of reasons, to which a request is often put asking 'when is the party?' Now we all know the person asking for the party has no intention or seriousness, it is a just a tiny little casual gesture to acknowledge the underlying reason of celebration. The 'host to be' wastes no time and replies 'anytime' to this question in the same breath without flapping an eyelid.

By this logic, the entire humanity owes us thousands of parties. Correct?

Readers Can Contribute

The characters and anecdotes covered in this book are the ones we all might have come across, albeit with a different degree of identification. The idea is to find humour in ordinary circumstances and look at the lighter side of life amidst unavoidable hustle-bustle and demanding chores. This is just the first serving of this book. There are many more interesting characters and anecdotes that I wish to cover in subsequent sequels of the book.

As readers you are welcome to contribute ideas / anecdotes / or characters for the sequel. You can do that in two ways:

In form of ideas / suggestions – the ideas will be developed by the author to make a full-fledged chapter out of it

In form of completely written chapters containing a well developed character sketch followed by anecdote(s) related to them. This form of submission may be directly edited and printed in the book. The chapter should contain minimum 2500 words to be considered for print. The submission will be acknowledged along with a brief coverage about the contributor.

No remuneration will be made for ideas or selected submission. This can be viewed as a platform for expression and finding an audience that can be enthralled by your creative side.

So remove your 'Human Microscopes' to observe the humour around you. All suggestions / criticisms / ideas and submissions can be e-mailed at jasjitanand@rediffmail.com.

ISBN   : 8188575682
Size   : 7.75" x 5.1"
Extent : 160pp
Binding : PB
Price   : ₹ 100

34 Bubblegums and Candies

Preeti Shenoy

These 34 real life incidents hide your story somewhere in between: some humorous, some moving or thought-provoking, some jolting, but each highlighting a flavor of life. Life has no "instruction manual" for the candies it offers, but let's chew the happy gum for a little more and swallow the ones we don't like.

Preeti is a bestselling author and has a unique take on life which is also reflected in her book *Life is What You Make It.*

ISBN   : 9789380349237
Size   : 7.75" x 5.1"
Extent : 224pp
Binding : PB
Price   : ₹ 100

Corporate Atyaachaar: …The comical journey of an office doormat

Abhay Nagarajan

A subservient 24-year-old financial advisor moves out of campus, to land straight under a dominating, obnoxious boss who has no confidence in his intellectual abilities. To top it, he has to play pal with a dancing dog which suffers from a memory loss, a nude art painter client, and many other frustrating specimen.

Abhay excels in comical representations of the world around, no thanks to his Master's in finance and all thanks to a healthy sense of humour.

ISBN : 9789380349312
Size : 7.75" x 5.1"
Extent : 184pp
Binding : PB
Price : ₹ 100

Beep You! You Beep Hole: the black book of Indian cuss & slurs

Smarak Swain

Ever wondered what those swearwords you use all the time mean? This book tries to do just that! Making sense of swearwords spoken across the length and breadth of the countries.

If you cuss frequently, this is a book for you. If you do not, you need to know why not, and this book is for you. If you don't do wither: eh…just $%^&＆ off!

Smarak is an IITian interested in applied psychology and film-making; this book stems from his interest in social issues.

ISBN : 9789382665144
Size : 7.75" x 5.1"
Extent : 184pp
Binding : PB
Price : ₹ 100

An Affair to Remember

Harkeerat Anand

Filled with cheesy motivational posters, computer workstations crammed side by side, bored employees and dumb bosses, ABCDEF Corp. is a boring Software Giant to be working in. Then enter a man and his best friend, and make everything topsy turvy, not before being flushed into chaos themselves too.

Peppy, wild, and bitterly sarcastic, this book is a humorous retelling of every person's story.

Harkeerat holds a Master's degree in Electronics Engineering and currently is a Ph.D. scholar at IIT Delhi.